"Aaagh!" everyone cried at once. Pillows flew at me from all directions, but I hardly felt them. I was still in a state of shock. We had been hired to throw a birthday party for one of our *classmates*—and not just any classmate, either. Casey Wyatt was the most obnoxious boy ever to pass through the halls of Canfield Middle School!

Ask your bookseller for these other PARTY LINE titles:

#1 ALLIE'S WILD SURPRISE

#3 BECKY'S SUPER SECRET (June, 1990)

#4 ROSIE'S POPULARITY PLAN (July, 1990)

Special party tips in every book!

JULIE'S BOY PROBLEM

by Carrie Austen

SPLASH™

A BERKLEY / SPLASH BOOK

THE PARTY LINE #2: JULIE'S BOY PROBLEM is an original publication of the Berkley Publishing Group. This work has never appeared before in book form.

A Berkley Book/published by arrangement with General Licensing Company, Inc.

PRINTING HISTORY
Berkley edition/April 1990

A GLC BOOK

Splash and *The Party Line* are trademarks of General Licensing Company, Inc.
Cover logo and design by James A. Lebbad.
Cover painting by Mike Wimmer.

ISBN: 0-425-12048-1
RL:4.4

A BERKLEY BOOK® TM 757,375
Berkley Books are published by The Berkley Publishing Group,
200 Madison Avenue, New York, New York 10016.
The name "BERKLEY" and the "B" logo
are trademarks belonging to Berkley Publishing Corporation.

PRINTED IN THE UNITED STATES OF AMERICA

10 9 8 7 6 5 4 3 2 1

JULIE'S BOY PROBLEM

One

"Hey, Rosie," I whispered to my best friend. "Doesn't Mark Harris look good today?"

She turned and rolled her eyes at me. "Yes, he does. Just like yesterday and the day before and the day before that. Now will you please shut up and pay attention?"

I shrugged. I couldn't help it. All I had been thinking about lately was how incredibly cute Mark was. Even though we were sitting in biology class and I was supposed to be taking notes, I kept sneaking looks across the room at Mark. I was trying to be cool about it, because I'd die if he ever suspected I liked him *that* way. Mark and I have kind of been buddies for a year or so, ever since we discovered we were both major Red Sox fans. When we talk, it's always been about games and stats and stuff like that. I don't know how I never managed to notice before how adorable he is.

But lately I haven't been able *not* to notice. He's like a younger version of River Phoenix. I mean, he's *that* cute.

Rosie nudged me and passed me a note. It read, "Hey, Berger, listen up!" and was signed "Becky and Allie." Becky Bartlett and Allison Gray are my two other best friends, besides Rosie. We're all in the seventh grade together, and biology is our absolute *least* favorite class.

They sit right behind me and Rosie, so I turned around and stuck out my tongue at them.

"Julie, is there something in the back of the room that the rest of us should know about?" Ms. Pernell asked.

I swiveled my head back toward the front of the room. "Uh, no," I said guiltily. "I thought I heard something." As I spoke, I could feel the most intense blush spreading across my face. I was so embarrassed—I knew Mark would be looking at me, because everyone in the class was. Although I'm a pretty good student, I get in trouble a lot because it's hard to be in class with your three best friends in the world and not talk all period!

"Well, why don't you just watch what I'm going to write on the board now," Ms. Pernell said in a slightly angry voice. She picked up her chalk and wrote our homework assignment on the blackboard.

"On Monday, we're going to begin our frog dissections," she announced, and a couple of kids in the class groaned. "It's nothing to worry about," Ms. Pernell went on. "We'll be working in pairs, the way all great researchers do." She chuckled as if she had just made the funniest joke in the world. Then she went to her desk and picked up her clipboard. "Now, let's see . . . Rick Addison, you will be working with Rosie Torres. Becky Bartlett, you'll be with . . ."

"I can't believe Mark Harris is my lab partner!" I cried. "This is the worst! I just know I'll freak when I have to touch that stupid frog!"

"Or when Mark sits next to you," Rosie joked. We were walking along the sidewalk on our way home after school. Usually we take the bus, but I made her walk with me that day because I couldn't talk about Mark with anyone else around. And I just *had* to talk about him.

"I just hope I don't do something incredibly dumb," I said.

"You won't," Rosie assured me, shifting her backpack from one shoulder to the other. "You're good at that kind of stuff. Remember how you used to do surgery on my dolls when their arms got broken?"

"Yeah." I smiled. "But they weren't all green and slimy. And they didn't have real guts and junk like that."

"Julie! Yuck!" Rosie wrinkled her nose in disgust.

"Rosie, don't make a face like that!"

"Why not? If you can say something so unbelievably gross, why can't I make a face?"

"Because," I said, "your face might freeze like that."

"Ha, ha." Rosie didn't think my joke was very funny.

"Sorry, just kidding. But really, you shouldn't do it because it can give you wrinkles."

"Get out, Julie. I never heard anything so dumb."

"It's true. Heather told me. She read it in some fashion magazine." Heather is my oldest sister and if anyone is a beauty expert, she is. She's eighteen—and totally gorgeous.

"Really, though, what am I going to do?" I asked Rosie. "I just know I'll do something stupid in bio."

"I think we should be more worried about what *Becky* is going to do. She can't even open her locker without help. Giving her a knife and a dead frog is really asking for trouble."

Rosie was right. Our friend Becky is so clumsy that her parents won't let her near any of the breakable stuff, like china and glassware, in the restaurant they own, the Moondance Café. It's as if there is some kind of jinx around her. At least I'm fairly coordinated. You really have to be if you're athletic, like I am. I'm pretty good at sports, especially baseball. Rosie's pretty coordinated, too. She has to be to polish her nails as perfectly as she does!

When we turned the corner, a group of about six boys from our class went riding past us on their bikes. Casey Wyatt, the most obnoxious boy in our class, was out in front making siren noises. Mark was in the group, too. "Oh no," I hissed to Rosie. "What if he heard me? I'll die!"

Rosie shook her head. "No way. He couldn't have."

Just then Casey made a sharp turn away from the group and nearly ran me over. What a creep!

"Hey, Berger!" he yelled. "Nice going in bio today!"

Rosie and I ignored him.

"What were you looking for in the back of the room, anyway?" Casey asked loudly. "A boyfriend?"

"No, I was looking for your brain," I said. "But I didn't see it anywhere."

Rosie burst out laughing. The other guys were waiting up for Casey, and they laughed, too—even Mark. I couldn't help smiling, even though Casey looked really mad.

"Hey, you're blinding me, tinsel teeth!" Casey yelled.

I shut my mouth immediately. I *hate* having braces. Leave it to that rotten Casey Wyatt to say the worst possible thing in the world. In front of Mark, too! I felt a horrible blush creeping over my face for the second time that day. I hoped Mark couldn't see it. He was circling around on his bike behind Casey, so I don't think he was looking at me. Rosie and I just kept walking, and I looked straight ahead.

"Let's get out of here," I heard Casey say. "We have better things to do than stand around talking to girls." With that, he turned his bike around and sped off down the street. The others followed. I had never thought I'd be glad to see Mark Harris disappear from sight, but that time I was.

"Casey Wyatt is such a—such a dweeb!" I shouted once they were out of earshot. "He makes me so mad!" I'd never give him the satisfaction of knowing how much his teasing upsets me. That wasn't the first time he'd said something mean, but it was definitely the worst. I felt awful.

"Just ignore him," said Rosie.

"Why do those other guys hang out with him?" I asked.

"I guess they think he's funny." Rosie shrugged. "He just hates girls."

"Well, I hate *him*," I said. I know that probably sounds a little extreme, but that's how I felt.

"Listen, I'll call you tomorrow," Rosie said when we reached my street. "And don't worry about the lab on Monday, okay?"

"Yeah, right. My braces are blinding, I don't want to touch a dead frog, and my lab partner is Mark Harris. What do I have to worry about?" I couldn't help being a little sarcastic. But Rosie was my friend and she was trying to cheer me up. "Okay, I won't worry. Thanks for listening, Rosie. See you later."

As soon as I walked in the door, my mother called out, "Julie? Is that you?" I swear, my mom can see through walls. No matter who comes in, she always knows who it is, even if she happens to be in another part of the house at the time.

"Yes, Mom, it's me." I dropped my books on

the bottom step of the stairway and wandered toward the kitchen. It was a mistake, though, because I had to pass through the dining room, which has a big mirror on one wall. I stopped in front of it and smiled at my reflection. My looks had never bothered me before, but now I felt like a big brace face. How could I ever expect Mark to fall in love with a metal mouth like me? Not that I really wanted him to fall in *love*, exactly. I just wouldn't mind if he fell in *like*. Couldn't they invent braces that you only had to wear for two weeks instead of two years?

Why couldn't I be beautiful like my older sisters? Maybe I'm going to improve with age, but that wasn't going to do me any good right then. The more I looked at myself, the worse I felt. It wasn't that I thought I was ugly. I just felt pitifully average. I have straight honey-blond hair and blue eyes, and I'm kind of on the skinny side. *Maybe I should give up sports,* I thought to myself. *Maybe then I'll look more like how a girl is supposed to look.*

"I can't believe it, Julie," my mother called from the kitchen. "You've been in the house for at least five minutes and you haven't started eating yet."

I went in and rummaged through the refrigerator, but I just didn't feel like eating anything. My cat, Dizzy, was in the kitchen, too, trying to get some milk for herself. She rubbed up against my legs and purred loudly.

"See anything that looks good?" my mom asked.

"Uh-uh," I said, squatting down to pick up Dizzy.

"What's wrong?" my mother asked. "Why do you look so tragic? Smile a little."

"I'm never going to smile again," I said dramatically. "I wouldn't want to blind anyone."

Mom motioned toward the table. "Sit down," she said. I plunked down on a chair, with Dizzy on my lap. "Don't you remember when Heather had braces?"

"No, not really," I said. "Did she wear them in her sleep or something?"

"No, silly. She had them when she was your age. But you probably don't remember them because you got so used to seeing them," my mother explained.

"Mom, do you expect me to believe that nobody notices I have braces?" I asked her.

"No, honey. It's just that they're not such a big deal," she said.

Not a big deal? I said to myself. Sometimes my mother doesn't know what she's talking about. "Mom, I'm going upstairs for a while," I said, standing up. I carried Dizzy upstairs to the bathroom and looked at my metallic smile in the mirror again.

"When you're trying to get Mark Harris to like you, braces are a very big deal," I told my cat. "You're just lucky you don't have any." Then I made a very important decision. From that moment on, I would open my mouth as little as possible in public.

I wouldn't even eat.

Two

I was doodling a heart shape in my loose-leaf notebook when the phone rang. Laurel—my fifteen-year-old sister, who practically lives on the telephone—got to it in record time.

"Julie! It's for you!" she called from the hallway outside our rooms. "It's Mrs. Wyatt!"

Mrs. Wyatt? I couldn't believe Casey's mother was calling me. Maybe there was another Wyatt family in Canfield. I thumped down the hall in my socks, and Laurel handed the phone to me.

"Don't stay on too long," she said. "I'm expecting a really important call."

"Okay, okay," I said. My sister is so unbelievable sometimes. She seems to think the phone is reserved for her private use. "Hello?" I said into the phone.

"Hello, Julie," said Mrs. Wyatt. "I ran into your mother at the supermarket yesterday and she was telling me about your party business. I wonder if you'd do a party for me. It's two weeks from this Saturday—the twenty-first."

Rosie, Becky, Allie, and I run our own business. It's called The Party Line. We throw parties for little kids, doing everything from buying the cake to dressing up as clowns. So far we've made pretty good money, and we have a lot of fun doing it, too. We have flyers posted in stores all over town, and our parents are pretty good at spreading the word about The Party Line among their friends.

"Sure," I said. "We'd love to. I just need some information from you—"

Mrs. Wyatt interrupted me, saying quickly, "My kids are all home from school right now so I can't really talk for long." I heard a loud shriek in the background. If the other Wyatt children were anything like Casey, I knew she had her hands full. "Can you—Susie, put that down! Excuse me, Julie. Can you do a party for boys?" she asked.

"Definitely," I said. "We did our very first party for Allison Gray's little brother, and it was a big hit."

"Oh, good, I'm glad to hear that. Listen, I have to run before these kids tear up my house," Mrs. Wyatt said with a laugh. "How about if I give you a call tomorrow evening and go over all the details? My husband should be home then and he can keep an eye on the little ones."

"Okay," I said, overwhelmed. If her children were that wild, I wasn't sure what we'd do with them—but business is business, and I knew we all could use the money. I said good-bye to Mrs. Wyatt and hung up.

I sat there in the hallway and thought about what a good idea The Party Line had been. It all started when we pitched in to help Allie's mom after the clown she hired for Jonathan's birthday party didn't show up. We ended up doing such a good job that someone wanted to hire us right away to do another party! Becky decided then and there that we should start our own business. Since it was her idea, she's the president of The Party Line—not that we're incorporated or anything, but we all have different jobs and we all contribute things to the parties.

Becky comes up with most of the ideas for the party themes. She's really creative. Of course, it's true that sometimes she's a little *too* creative. For example, she once used food coloring to make a snack look more interesting, and we ended up with blue onion dip. Most of her ideas are pretty terrific, though. Because her parents run a café, she knows a lot about fixing food, so she usually takes care of deciding about the menus, too.

Allie is vice president, and she takes care of all the little details. She's incredibly organized, and she fills out an information sheet every time we're hired to give a party so that we don't forget anything. I guess you could say she's a perfectionist—only she's not always perfect. For our first official money-making job, she forgot to figure in a profit for us on her information sheet, and we almost ended up doing the party for free! Allie is also a real music freak. She's crazy about the rock singer Vermilion, and the high point of her whole life was when she and Becky got to meet Vermilion and go to the concert she did here in Canfield. Allie's a pretty good singer herself. She gets nervous about singing in front of other people, but since that concert she's been trying to get over her shyness. Whenever she sings for the little kids, they love it. We're always trying to get her to sing in something at school, but she says she's not ready yet.

Rosie, however, is always ready for anything—and everything! She's a great dresser, and she can make all kinds of costumes. She's great with makeup, too. She's given us a lot of good funny faces for the parties, and every time we pass a cosmetic counter at the mall one of us ends up with a temporary makeover. Rosie is also an incredible artist. She can draw really well, and she designed our flyer. She's our treasurer, too, and she keeps track of all our money. If you ask me, Rosie does more than anyone else—but I'm probably just saying that because she's my *best* best friend.

I'm officially the secretary, which means I have to take notes when we have meetings. Usually I just doodle in my notebook, and then try to remember later what we talked about if anyone asks me. Since I'm into sports, I'm in charge of any physical activities we do at parties, like games and softball and even dancing. I make different cassette tapes for each party, and I try to customize them so they fit in with the theme. Playing D.J. is probably my favorite part. My sisters tease me about it, but I figure I'll be a famous radio announcer someday and then they'll be sorry.

Speaking of sisters, I had just picked up the phone to call Allie—the next person on the telephone chain we set up to let us all know about important Party Line news—when Laurel came out of her room. "Julie, can you *please* get off the phone?" she whined.

"I hardly ever use the phone," I complained. "Can't you let me use it just once without asking me to get off?"

She sighed loudly. "I know, Julie, but I'm

waiting for this really important call. I wouldn't ask you unless—"

"I just have to make one short call," I promised. "Then you can talk to anyone you want." She slammed her door, and I dialed Allie's number. It was exactly eight o'clock, the official time we use to call each other about Party Line business. We invented the telephone chain partly to deal with people like bossy older sisters. This way, I call Allie, she calls Becky, and Becky calls Rosie; we all know what's going on, and no one has to spend all night on the phone. We try to do it between eight and nine o'clock at night.

Allie answered the phone. "Hello?"

"We have another job!" I blurted out.

She squealed happily on the other end of the phone. "Who's the client?"

"Mrs. Wyatt. Listen, I can't stay on the phone," I whispered as Laurel opened her door just a crack. "My sister is having a fit waiting for some guy to call her."

"Okay, I'll pass it on," said Allie. "What day is the party?"

"The twenty-first," I said. "Talk to you later!" I hung up and grinned at Laurel. "Okay, the line is clear for Mr. Wonderful," I teased her.

But when the phone rang five minutes later and Laurel ran to get it, it wasn't Mr. Wonderful. It was Rosie, and Laurel practically threw the phone at me. Rosie is just before me in the chain, so I knew a second chain had started.

"What's up?" I asked her.

"Becky called an emergency meeting. You know Becky—she has to act like the president once in a while."

"You mean bossy?" I said, giggling.

"Exactly," Rosie agreed. "She says this new job is important and it shouldn't wait until our regular meeting on Sunday. So there's a meeting of The Party Line at two o'clock tomorrow, in her attic."

"See you then!" I told Rosie.

Three

"Tell us! Tell us!" said Allie, tossing me my favorite pink pillow.

Our meetings for The Party Line are always held in Becky's attic. It's a huge room that her mom lets us use. Becky and Allie did most of the fixing up, pushing old trunks and boxes against the walls so that we could sit in the middle of the room. Then all of us did the "interior decorating." We fixed it up with pictures of rock musicians and movie stars and a few of Becky's animal posters. Each of us contributed something to sit on, like an old rug or a cushion, and we keep collecting more.

"So what's this about Mrs. Wyatt's party?" said Becky, stretching out on a small pink and blue hooked rug.

A bowl of potato chips sat in the middle of our circle. I reached for one and practiced eating while only opening my mouth a crack. It didn't work very well, but I knew I'd get better. Then I began to explain about the phone call, still trying to keep my mouth closed. "Mishus Wyatt called me."

"Casey Wyatt's mother, right?" asked Allie.

"Yesh," I replied.

"Julie, what's the matter with your mouth?" Becky looked at me, puzzled.

"I'm practishing shpeaking without showing my brashes," I explained. "The party's for Casey's little brother—I don't know his name. Mrs. Wyatt is calling me tonight to give me all the details. I hope he's not anything like his big brother!" I said slowly, barely moving my lips.

"Julie!" Rosie cried. "I can't believe you!"

"Okay, okay. I'll talk with my mouth open." I sighed. "Even though I look like a total geek."

"It's not that, stupid!" Rosie said. "Casey Wyatt doesn't *have* a brother!"

"*What?*"

"Rosie's right," Allie said matter-of-factly. "Three little sisters, but no brothers."

"They must have broken the mold," Becky joked.

"But wait a minute, you guys," I said, a sinking feeling in the pit of my stomach. "Mrs.

Wyatt said the party was for boys. I know she did."

"You know what this means, don't you?" said Allie.

"Yup!" said Rosie, picking up a big flowered pillow and throwing it at me. "If we're doing a party for Mrs. Wyatt's son, it's for—"

"Casey Wyatt!" I screamed just as the pillow landed in my lap.

"Aaagh!" everyone cried at once. Pillows flew at me from all directions, but I hardly felt them. I was still in a state of shock. We had been hired to throw a birthday party for one of our class-mates—and not just any classmate, either. Casey Wyatt was the most obnoxious boy ever to pass through the halls of Canfield Middle School.

"What do we do now?" asked Rosie. "We've only done parties for little kids."

"We can't do it," I said. "We can't throw a party for boys our age!"

Allie looked confused. "Why not?" she asked. "I mean, what's the difference?"

"*Al*-lison!" I groaned.

"We just have to approach it as a business deal," said Becky in her take-charge voice. "We agreed to help Mrs. Wyatt, and now we have to go through with it." She was right, of course, but that didn't make me feel any better.

"I'm sorry, you guys. I really messed up," I said. "I should have asked her more about the party on the phone."

"It's okay, Julie. Anybody could make the same mistake. Hey, I get excited when I think about making money, too!" Rosie said, smiling. "Besides, we never really thought that a customer would want us to do a party for a kid our age."

"That's true," Allie agreed.

I shook my head. "I still have a horrible feeling about this."

"What's the big deal?" said Becky. "We'll survive."

"The big deal is," I told her, "Casey hangs around with a lot of the guys in our class—including Mark Harris. They're always together, and you know he'll be there." My friends knew all about my crush on Mark, so I figured I didn't need to tell them just how bad the situation was.

Rosie kneeled next to me on her threadbare Oriental rug. "Listen," she said, "this may turn out great. Maybe now, for Mark's sake, you'll finally let me give you that new look." Rosie just never gave up trying to get me to give in to a permanent makeover.

"Sure. You can make me invisible," I answered.

"Julie, look at it this way," said Allie. "You'll be working at the party, so you won't have to worry about talking to Mark."

Sometimes it is so frustrating to talk to Allie about boys. I like her a lot, but I just wish she were a little more mature. She and Becky are light-years behind Rosie and me when it comes to clothes and boys and stuff like that.

"Allie," I patiently explained, "I'll be running around serving things and working up a sweat. My hair will probably be a mess after the first twenty minutes, and then I'll look at him, and I'll blush my famous blush—you know, all the way up to my hair! And then Casey will say, 'Hey, metal mouth! Are you feeling all right?' " I knew I sounded a little hysterical, but I just couldn't help it. It was terrible!

"Take it easy," said Rosie, gently grabbing my arm. "If you're really worried about how you look, wear something light and loose, like your big blue striped shirt, so you'll keep cool. And I can put your hair up for you so it won't get messy. You'll be fine, Julie, honest. We'll all be there. We'll all help you."

Good old Rosie. She always understands me, even though I tend to go off the deep end when

I get really worried about something. "Thanks, Rosie. I guess it's not the end of the world," I admitted with a small smile.

"That's the spirit," said Becky with a smile. Allie nodded encouragingly.

But deep down inside, I knew this party was going to make me wish we had never invented The Party Line!

Four

We decided that the emergency meeting on Saturday took the place of our regular Party Line meeting, so on Sunday we rode our bikes to Van Fleet Park instead. It was sunny and warm and the park was crowded with all kinds of people. We passed the duck pond and took the path past the picnic area, where little kids were running around playing tag. As we passed the baseball diamond, some boys were just starting a game.

"Let's watch for a minute," I said, coasting to a stop. I got off my bike and laid it down on the grass.

"Typical," said Rosie. "I should have known we couldn't go to the park without doing some major boy-watching."

I grinned. "You know me so well."

Allie and Becky had ridden on ahead, and they came back to join us. "What's going on?" asked Allie.

"Some of the boys in our class are playing," explained Rosie.

I recognized Alex Wishinsky, Peter Wheeler, and Kip Mason.

"Hi!" called Peter, waving his glove at us.

"Hi," I answered. We walked over closer, and I could see they were short a few players. "Need help?" I called.

"Sure," said Peter.

Back in elementary school, Peter and I had played baseball together every day during recess. Of course, that was before everyone started acting all weird about boys and girls playing together. I even had the home run record for a few weeks in fifth grade, until Alex broke it. My friends didn't play much and neither did my sisters, so the only chance I got was when the boys didn't mind including me in their games. Sometimes my father and I would go to the park together and just practice pitching and batting.

I looked at Allie and then at Becky. "Go ahead," Becky urged me. "We'll watch your bike."

I ran over to Peter, and he tossed me a glove. "Can you handle third base?"

"Sure," I said. I usually like to pitch, but I wasn't going to complain. As I trotted out to third, I glanced around the field. I didn't know all of the boys; some of them probably went to school in the next town over. And some of them were pretty cute! But I forced myself to pay attention to the game.

The pitcher wound up and let one fly, but it was a pretty slow pitch and the batter smacked it right to me. I scooped it off the ground easily, and fired the ball to first base with all my strength.

"Out!" cried Alex at first base.

The batter shook his head and trudged back to the bench.

"All right, Julie!" screamed Rosie.

"Way to go!" whooped Allie.

When the next batter approached the plate, I heard a commotion on the other side of the field, just past where my friends were sitting. It sounded like more boys were coming to play.

The next batter let two pitches go by before he took a swing. Then he drilled a shot to left field over my head. I knew this was going to be an extra-base hit, and I watched the boy behind me chase the ball. When he finally got it, he wheeled around and threw it to me, just as the runner came around second. I positioned myself right in the middle of the base path, and when the boy—who looked like he'd been lifting weights—ran right at me I just held out the ball and touched him with it. He was out! But he plowed into me anyway.

I hit the ground, hard. It hurt, but I was used to playing rough and I got up right away. As I was brushing the dirt off my shirt and jeans, Peter called, "Nice play, Julie!"

"Whoa—what did I just hear?" a familiar voice called out. "Is that a *girl* out there?"

I shaded my eyes from the sun and looked over at the sidelines. It was the birthday boy himself, Casey Wyatt. And with him was Mark Harris, as usual. *Oh, great,* I thought. *I've got dirt all over me, and I'm sure I looked like an idiot, letting that enormous Little Leaguer knock me over like that.* I scuffed the ground with my sneaker and hoped Mark wouldn't notice me.

But Casey wasn't about to let me off the hook. "How come you let a girl play?" he asked the other guys.

"Why shouldn't we?" Peter replied.

"Because I don't play baseball with girls," Casey said. "They stink."

"Actually, Julie is pretty good," Alex said in my defense. "She got the last two outs."

Will everybody please stop saying my name? I thought. I felt like disappearing. But it didn't look as though a big hole was going to open up under third base and swallow me.

"I have to go, anyway," I said quietly. I walked off the field and tossed the glove on the bench. I could tell Mark was looking at me, but I avoided him.

Peter ran over to me. "You don't have to leave, you know," he said.

"I know. But it won't be any fun for me with Casey around."

Peter nodded. "Sorry," he said under his breath.

"Thanks for letting me play," I told him. Then I joined Rosie, Becky, and Allie under a big oak tree where they were sitting.

"You were great out there," said Rosie. "Casey is such a jerk."

"Yeah," Allie agreed. "We could tell that the other guys wanted you to stay."

"Let's just get out of here," I said. "I don't want to see Casey Wyatt gloating."

We got on our bikes and headed to the other side of the park. I pedaled as hard as I could. I thought if I rode really fast, I could get rid of all the bad feelings inside me. *At least he didn't call me tinsel teeth,* I said to myself. But it didn't make me feel any better. That was the second time I had been embarrassed in front of Mark in three days. He was probably going to ask Ms. Pernell for a new lab partner!

Allie pulled up beside me, panting. "Are you sure we should do this party for Casey?" she asked.

"We have to," I said. "We promised Mrs. Wyatt."

We spent the rest of the afternoon hanging out in the park. After we rode our bikes around some more, we stopped and bought ice cream cones at the snack stand. I got my favorite flavor, mint chocolate chip.

"Feeling better?" Rosie asked me as we wandered over to the picnic area to sit down and eat our cones.

"Yeah," I admitted. From where we were sitting, we could see the ducks and geese on the other side of the pond. Some boys were skipping rocks across the water. We ignored them until we heard some of the ducks squawking.

"What are they doing?" asked Becky, standing to get a better view.

"I think they're trying to scare the birds," said Rosie, just as one of the geese took wing and flew away. "And it looks like they're succeeding."

"We'd better go stop them," said Becky. She's into animal rights and stuff like that. She won't stand for any animal being mistreated.

We took off on our bikes, but just as we got close enough to see the boys, a park ranger's truck drove up. The ranger got out and told the boys either to stop misbehaving or to leave the park immediately.

"That's Casey, isn't it?" Becky asked me.

I nodded.

"I should have known," she said. "Wherever there's trouble, he isn't far away. I knew he was a rat, but I didn't know he hated birds, too."

"Looks like this is going to be the toughest party ever," said Allie, with a tiny smile.

Five

I stared at the frog in front of me. Was I really supposed to cut the slimy thing open?

Mark handed me a knife. "I hope you're not squeamish," he said.

I didn't know what to do next. Ms. Pernell had given us a detailed list of instructions, but they didn't say anything about how to dissect a frog when the boy you were standing next to made your knees weak. "No, you do it," I told Mark, handing him the knife.

"Are you sure?" he asked me, grinning.

I nodded shyly. I was determined not to smile in front of him, not at this close range.

Mark made a small incision down the front of the frog. He seemed to be pretty good at it. He looked just like the surgeons on all those hospital soap operas.

Ms. Pernell came over to our table. "Nice

work, you two," she said. "Don't forget to draw your diagram of the frog's internal organs."

I wrinkled my nose. This dissection was only going to get worse. I glanced across the room at Rosie. I could just imagine what kind of diagram she would draw. They'd probably end up framing it and hanging it in the science lab for everyone to see.

Mark continued cutting the frog, then peeled back its skin. Actually, it didn't look too bad inside. It smelled really strongly of chemicals, though. A few tables over, one boy made a gagging sound and ran out of the room, holding his hand over his mouth.

"I guess he doesn't like blood and guts," Mark whispered, and I giggled.

I picked up my pencil and started trying to identify the various body parts of the frog. "What's that?" I asked Mark, confused.

"A fly he ate for his last meal?" he suggested, and we both cracked up again.

Out of the corner of my eye, I saw Casey raise his hand.

"Yes, Casey?" said Ms. Pernell with a sigh. She'd had Casey in her class long enough to know that he was always up to something.

"Are you sure these frogs are really dead?" asked Casey.

"Yes, Casey. They most certainly are dead.

They came to us frozen, in fact." Ms. Pernell looked at Casey over the rims of her glasses.

"Well, okay," Casey said slowly. Then he went back to dissecting.

About a minute later, he shouted, "Hey! My frog is still alive!" Something shiny and green jumped across the room.

"Ribbet," the frog croaked. It sounded like a big bullfrog, but I couldn't see from my seat. "Ribbet!" it said again, even louder.

Ms. Pernell's glasses dropped off her nose. The frog jumped again, and a couple of kids shrieked and pulled their feet up on their chairs.

"Casey Wyatt, go to the principal's office *immediately*!" Ms. Pernell yelled.

"But I didn't do anything," he said. "I'm telling you, my frog wasn't dead!"

All of a sudden I thought back to the day before, when the boys had been playing around the duck pond. Since Casey knew we were going to begin our dissections the next day, he'd probably caught a frog in the park. I was surprised he would put so much planning into a silly prank.

"March! Now!" Ms. Pernell ordered Casey. As he strolled out the door, he turned around and winked at the rest of the class.

Alex Wishinsky caught the frog out in the hallway and put it in a box so he could return it to the pond. Mark and I went back to our lab table.

"Well, if our frog wasn't dead before, he is now," Mark said. He smiled and I felt like melting.

"Definitely," I said. "So what's that squiggly thing?"

Later that afternoon, I was getting some books out of my locker to take home when Mark came walking up the corridor. We'd had a really good time together in frog lab, and I figured this was a good chance for me to talk to him, alone.

"Hi, Mark," I said.

"Oh, hi, Julie," he answered. He opened his locker, which was about ten feet away from mine.

I took a deep breath. "I wanted to ask you about the bio homework. Does she—"

"Hey, Mark, what's up?" said Casey, scuffling toward us. I could have killed him. Of all the people to interrupt my first real conversation with Mark!

"Not much. What's up with you?" Mark replied. "You look kind of bummed."

"Well, you're not going to believe this, but my mom hired some dorky party outfit to throw a birthday party for me," Casey said glumly.

I gulped and stuck my head into my locker, pretending to look for something.

"What's so terrible about that?" asked Mark.

"I'm too old for that kid stuff," Casey said, frowning. "It's going to be so lame. What if there's a clown handing out party favors or something?"

"It won't be like that," said Mark. "Your mom probably just needs someone to help her with the food and stuff."

"Then the food will probably stink, too. It'll be like the stuff you get at weddings—vegetables and some kind of dippy dip." The scorn in Casey's voice was unmistakable. "And wimpy cake that tastes like sawdust with toothpaste icing." Casey's voice was getting louder and angrier. "What are they gonna do? Decorate the cake with little flowers? And hang balloons around the place?"

"I'm sure your mom knows what you like and what you don't like," Mark said. "Your party last year was okay. Your mom is trying to do something nice for you—give her a break."

"Yeah, I guess so." Casey tapped his fingers against a locker. "I just hope the guys don't think it's totally stupid."

"It'll be great, Case. And if it isn't, we can always go outside and play ball or something," Mark suggested.

What a great idea! I said to myself. *If they spend the whole time outside, I won't be able to embarrass myself in front of Mark.* I was ready to slam my locker and call it a day, and I was supposed to be meeting everyone out front. But I was afraid that if I moved, Casey would notice me and start teasing me.

He had relaxed a little, though. I was impressed by how easily Mark had convinced him that the party wasn't going to be all bad—and I was grateful, too.

"Let's get our bikes," said Mark. He and Casey started walking away and I breathed a sigh of relief. I stepped back from my locker and shut it quietly.

"Bye, Julie!" Mark called from halfway down the hall.

"Uh, bye, Mark," I said. I'd thought he had completely forgotten that I was standing there.

"See you later, metal mouth!" Casey shouted.

I cringed. So much for my first encounter with Mark.

"Let's walk," I said. "We need to talk and we can't do it on the bus." We were standing around in the parking lot, and I had just told everyone about the conversation I had overheard between Casey and Mark.

"You want to *walk*?" said Becky. "With this

load of books?" She slung her book bag over her shoulder and groaned under the weight of it.

"We'd better," said Allie, flipping her long brown hair over her shoulder. "Julie's right. We have to plan the boys' party very carefully, and we don't want anyone to hear us. I'll help you carry your stuff, Becky."

"Thanks." Becky took a few books out of her book bag and handed them to Allie. We started walking up the street, away from school.

"Maybe Casey doesn't like this party idea, but at least he doesn't know who's doing it yet," said Rosie. "If he found out we were the people his mom hired, it would be the absolute worst!"

"By the time he finds out," added Becky, "he'll be having such a good time he won't care."

"I sure hope so," I said. "I wish I could turn back the clock to the time I got the phone call that got us into this mess."

"It doesn't matter," said Rosie.

"What do you mean, 'It doesn't matter'?" I asked.

"Just that. Julie, even if you could go back, you'd probably do the same thing again."

"Are you nuts, Rosie?"

"No. Think about it. We're a business. It's our job to do parties. We can't pick and choose. That's discrimination. If Mrs. Wyatt called and asked us to do a party, we have to do it. And we owe her the best party we can give," she explained.

Casey's party was the Saturday after next. I wished the time would fly by, so that the party would be over and done with and I could stop being a nervous wreck. "How are we supposed to figure out what Casey wants for his party?" I wailed.

"Well, we know what Casey *doesn't* want," said Allie. "Why don't we start with that?"

"Good idea," said Rosie.

"Okay," said Becky. "He doesn't want any kid stuff. And Julie said he liked Mark's idea about going outside to play ball. Why don't we make the party outside? I know, let's have a baseball game!"

That's why Becky is president of The Party Line. She always comes through with the best ideas.

"I can probably borrow stuff from my brothers," Allie said.

"I can bring my glove and my dad's glove. We have a bat and ball, too," I said.

"I can borrow David's glove and bat," added Becky. "And Russell has a glove." David is Becky's fifteen-year-old brother, and Russell is her stepfather.

"Do you think we can have the party at Melrose Field?" asked Rosie. Melrose Field is a piece of land the Melrose family donated to the town years ago so there would be a place to have town picnics and other outdoor events, like Canfield's annual Fourth of July softball game.

"That's a great idea!" I said. Melrose Field is a lot more private than the park, and it has a really nice baseball diamond. "I'll check it out and see if we can reserve it."

"What about the food?" asked Allie.

"They don't want fancy food. I think they want food they recognize. You know, regular food. And no bakery cake—Casey says it tastes like sawdust with toothpaste icing," I said, giggling in spite of myself.

"I hate to admit it, but Casey *can* be pretty funny sometimes," Rosie said.

"It's true," Allie said. "I mean, he *is* a major pain. But if you could have seen the look on Kip Mason's face when that frog leaped onto his desk. . . ."

"I know, I know," I said. "I just wish he wasn't always trying to be funny at my expense!"

"I know how you feel," Becky said sympathetically. "I get just as mad as you do when he picks on your braces. Sometimes I think if I hear him make one more crack, *pow!*" Becky made a big fist and swung it around.

"Becky, my hero!" I said dramatically.

Becky looked a little embarrassed. "Well, he makes me mad, too! Anyway, back to business."

"Casey wants normal food," I reminded her.

"Leave that up to me," said Becky. "I'll figure it out."

I wished I were a little more confident of Becky's ability to plan the food. Most of the time she has good ideas, but like I said before, sometimes she tries things that are really wacky. One St. Patrick's Day she went a little wild with the green theme at the Moondance Café, and one of the customers almost fainted when she poured green cream into her coffee!

Becky must have seen the worried look on my face, because she said, "Don't worry, Julie. I'll run everything by you first." Then she giggled. "Although I wouldn't mind serving Casey some worm pie with a big helping of brussels sprouts ice cream!"

We all screamed and laughed. Only Becky could even imagine such a grisly combination. I knew I could count on my friends to put on a terrific party—even if it was for a boy we didn't like.

Six

We spent the next few days finishing up our party plans. Everything went a lot better than I expected.

"This is great!" I said, reading Becky's shopping list. "Hot dogs with sauerkraut, roasted peanuts, caramel corn, potato chips, macaroni salad, ice cream, and cans of cold soda. I love it!"

"No boy can say that's wimpy food," said Becky. "It's totally ballpark."

Allie had a good idea, too. She thought we could give out baseball caps to all the guests instead of party favors. "They can be red and blue," she said, "for the two teams."

"Excellent," I told her.

"What about baseball cards?" said Becky. "When David was thirteen, he had about a million of them and he used to sort through them every night with his friends."

"Can we afford both the hats and the cards?" asked Rosie. Since she's the treasurer, she's always thinking about our money and how we should spend it.

"I think so," I said. "We should have extra money because we don't have to spend anything on decorations or a birthday cake. And the baseball cards are like party favors. The only thing we have to spend money on is food, so I think we can afford the caps."

"Okay," said Rosie.

When I called Mrs. Wyatt that night to bring her up to date on the party, she was thrilled.

"Why, Julie, I think that all sounds wonderful. The boys will love it!" she said. "If you need extra money for those caps, just let me know. You girls are doing a terrific job so far," she added.

"Thanks, Mrs. Wyatt," I said. I guessed Casey hadn't told her yet how *he* felt about the party!

Wednesday after school we went over to On Track, the sporting goods store in the mall. We found some caps for only $2.50 each and decided we could include them in the price of the party.

For a while, things were moving along beautifully. Mark and I were still lab partners, our frog was still dead, and even though I wasn't exactly making him fall in love with me, he didn't seem to think I was a total zero, either. I couldn't believe I'd been so worried about one stupid party.

"Ugh—what *is* this?" exclaimed Becky. She poked at the casserole on her plate. It was Thursday, and we were eating lunch in the cafeteria.

"I don't know," said Rosie, "but I'm not touching it." She took a bite of a brownie and sipped her milk.

"You'll be hungry later," Allie told her. Then she looked at my plate. "You know this stuff is bad when even Julie doesn't want it." My humongous appetite was a favorite topic of conversation for my friends, especially at lunchtime.

"I'm not hungry," I said. That wasn't really true. I was starving, and even if I didn't like the mystery main course, I'd bought a yogurt, too: my favorite flavor, tropical fruit. But Mark was sitting at the next table, and I was too nervous to eat in front of him. What if something got stuck in my braces? "I had a big breakfast," I said.

"Well, I still think it's weird," said Allie. "You always have a big breakfast, and that's never stopped you from having a big lunch on top of it."

"Have a bite of my brownie," offered Rosie.

Before I could tell them that I was not going to eat anything no matter what they said, Casey's voice drifted over from the next table. He was being loud, as usual.

Rosie and I stared at each other as we listened to Casey say, "I found out who's doing the stupid party. Boy, I'd really like to meet those idiots. I'd tell them what I think of them."

I thought my heart was going to stop beating right there in the middle of the lunchroom.

"So who are they?" asked Mark, his head tilted back as he drained the last of his milk out of the carton.

"They call themselves The Party Line. Isn't that the stupidest name you've ever heard?"

Mark nearly choked on his milk.

"What's wrong with you?" said Casey.

"They're sitting right behind you," Mark told him. He turned and pointed to me. "Ask Julie. She can tell you all about The Party Line."

I held my social studies textbook in front of

my face, which I could feel beginning to heat up. I could tell that everyone at Mark and Casey's table was looking at me.

"What?" Casey cried, standing up. "*You're* doing the party?"

I put my book down slowly. Forgetting my braces for a second, I grinned. "Yeah. Me, Rosie, Becky, and Allie."

Alex and Kip and some other boys started laughing, and this time Casey was the one who blushed. I actually felt sorry for him for a second or two.

"Don't worry, we do terrific parties," I added.

Some of the other boys started laughing, and I knew that I had said the wrong thing.

"I don't want any gruesome girls throwing a party for me!" Casey complained. "Girls don't know how to do anything! You couldn't possibly give a good party!"

I jumped up. "That's the dumbest thing I ever heard of in my life! Girls can do anything boys can do, and probably even better!"

"Yeah!" shouted Becky. "And if we say we're planning a great party, then it'll *be* a great party."

"Yeah, right. Your idea of fun is probably singing queer songs and playing kissing games. Why don't you stick to dolls?" Casey said angrily.

"I've never had a doll!" I yelled back. "But if you want us to bring some to your party, we will!"

Elvin Schneider roared with laughter, and I could see Casey getting even more furious. Then Ms. Oliver hurried over to see what all the shouting was about.

I didn't care if I got in trouble. Who did he think he was, anyway, telling us we couldn't do something just because we were girls? I was standing with my hands on my hips, glaring at Casey.

Rosie took me by the arm. "Julie, remember, this is a job. We have to keep cool," she reminded me.

"Yeah," said Allie. "C-Casey will c-calm down when he gets used to the idea." I could tell she was nervous about the whole scene because she was stammering a little. She only does that when she's really worried about something, and I felt bad that I'd made her so upset.

"Sorry, you guys," I said. "I'll shut up now."

Why did Mark have to tell Casey we were giving the party, anyway? Well, one thing was for sure: he was hardly going to like me after the way I'd just acted. He was one of Casey's best friends, and I had insulted Casey. I knew that if anyone tried to bad-mouth Rosie, I'd automatically hate that person.

So I'd made Casey mad and looked bad in front of Mark. And I hadn't even eaten any lunch.

It was definitely not my day.

Seven

"So did you tell Mrs. Wyatt how much Casey hated the idea of us giving him a party?" Rosie asked me on the school bus the next morning.

"Well . . . not exactly," I said.

"What did you say?"

"I told her that he found out it was us, and that he wasn't too psyched."

"And what did she say?" asked Rosie.

"She said, and I quote, 'Don't worry. I'm sure Casey will get over it. He'll have a great time at the party.' " I shrugged.

"Good," said Rosie. "We can't cancel this party now. We've spent too much money—and time—on it."

"Uh-oh," I said as the bus pulled to a stop. "Here comes the birthday boy."

The doors swung open and Casey and a few of his friends got on the bus. When he walked past me and Rosie, Casey said, "Well, if it isn't the gruesome girls!"

His friends snickered.

"Look out, Becky," I said loudly, turning around in my seat. "Here come the beastly boys."

We all laughed at the nickname as Casey made his way to the back of the bus to sit with the other boys.

Allie leaned forward and whispered, "So what did Mrs. Wyatt say about the fact that Casey hates us?"

"She said Casey is just being his usual impossible self, and not to listen to him. She also said his bark is worse than his bite." I grinned.

"Well, I'm not getting close enough to Casey to find out," said Becky, shuddering at the thought.

"His bark is worse than his bite, huh?" said Rosie. "You know, I always did think he was a dog!"

We cracked up laughing.

"Look, the gruesome girls made a joke!" Casey yelled from the back of the bus. "I didn't know they knew any jokes."

"You're the joke, Casey!" I shouted back. "Just looking at you makes us laugh."

"Oh, yeah?" Casey shot back. "Well, every time you laugh, I can see my reflection in all that shiny metal on your teeth—and believe me, I look a lot better than you do!"

I gritted my teeth and glared at Casey. I don't think it's fair to make fun of things kids have to wear. It wasn't my fault my teeth weren't straight. That remark was the sort of low blow I could expect from a dweeb like Casey, though.

I kept quiet for the rest of the ride to school. Becky, Allie, and Rosie were talking about a movie they wanted to see that weekend. I just stared out the window.

In English class that day, it became clear that Casey wasn't going to forget our quarrel. In fact, he seemed determined to turn it into an all-out feud.

When I sat down at my desk, there was a note on my chair that said, "Reserved for gruesome girls." "Look at this," I said to Rosie.

"Ha, ha," she said in an annoyed voice. "Look, there's a piece of paper on my chair, too." In big red letters someone had written, "Gruesome girls should stick to babysitting."

"They're so immature," said Rosie. "But if that's the way they want to be, we can fight back." Her dark green eyes twinkled mischievously.

"What do you mean?" I asked.

"Shh," she said, pointing to the front of the

room. Our teacher, Ms. Lombardi, had just arrived.

"Good morning," she said. "Today we're going to continue our discussion of *The Pearl*."

Rosie took out her notebook and began writing something in it. She looked like she was taking the neatest notes, and I was impressed. How could she concentrate on John Steinbeck? All I could think about was how we were going to get revenge on the boys.

But at the end of class, she handed me a sheet of paper. On it was a song titled "Ode to the Beastly Boys." It went like this:

> Beastly boys are loathsome
> They eat worms and dirt
> But they run right to Mommy
> Whenever they get hurt.
>
> Beastly boys are ugly
> They make me want to barf
> They remind me of my puppy
> When I see them I think, "Arf!"
>
> Beastly boys are stupid
> Their brains are oh so small
> And when they open up their mouths
> They have no brains at all!

I burst out laughing as we walked down the corridor to math class. "Rosie, this is great! Now all we have to do is get Allie to perform it!"

"Perform what?" asked Allie, coming up behind us.

" 'Ode to the Beastly Boys,' " replied Rosie. She struck a pose. "My grand composition."

Becky giggled. "Let me see!"

When we walked into math, we were still laughing about the song Rosie had written. I couldn't believe how funny it was.

"Look, it's the giggling gruesome girls!" Elvin called out.

"Hey, Julie, where's your doll?" added Alex.

We took our seats without saying anything. Then Becky picked up a dustball from the floor.

"Oh, look!" she said loudly. "It's Alex's brain!"

"And here's Elvin's," added Allie, handing her a tiny scrap of paper.

"You'll have to hold onto these," said Becky, brushing off her hands so that the stuff flew off toward the boys. "You might need them sometime."

At lunchtime, I was prepared for another attack from the boys. But we had our song ready and I wasn't going to let them call us names without getting them back just as good. I was almost hoping the whole thing would turn into a food fight. Food fights are gross and messy, but boy, would I ever love to smash a plateful of the cafeteria's mystery special into Casey Wyatt's face!

Instead, Coach Piper, who's the head of the athletic department, got up to make an announcement. "Next week we will hold the annual Canfield Middle School fitness test," he said. "No one is required to compete, but everyone is eligible. Awards will be given for the best performances in each event. And every student who completes the basic requirements will earn a certificate of fitness."

"What do we have to do?" one kid called out.

"I was just getting to that," said Coach Piper. "The seven events are: sit-ups, chin-ups, push-ups, the hundred-yard dash, the broad jump, the softball throw, and the mile run. You may sign up in the gym, or you may sign up now. I have a handout describing what will be expected of you in each event."

Coach Piper didn't get to say anything more because everyone rushed to the middle of the cafeteria, where he was standing on a chair. Rosie and I ran up right away, and tried to make our way through the crowd to the sign-up sheet.

"What are *you* doing here?"

I rolled my eyes. Casey was right beside us in line.

"We're signing up for the fitness test," Rosie told him.

"Girls aren't invited," he said, grinning. "This is for boys only."

I shook my head. "That's not true! Coach Piper said every student could participate."

"Yeah, but he meant every *boy* student," Casey said.

Fortunately, we reached the front of the line just as the argument was heating up. "What's the problem?" asked Coach Piper.

Casey stuck out his chin. "These girls are trying to horn in on the guys' territory. Tell them, Coach. This is just for boys."

The coach smiled. "Sorry, Casey, but the competition is coed."

Casey looked as if he had just been hit on the head. He muttered something under his breath.

As Rosie and I wrote our names down on the sheet, Elvin yelled, "Give it up, girls! You can't compete with guys. Everyone knows that."

Casey said, "You wouldn't want to ruin your outfits by running in a race, would you?"

Jon Dolger added, "Go have a tea party, girls. We'll call you when the race is over."

I exchanged looks with Rosie. She's a really good runner, and I knew she was going to blow away some of the guys. I was pretty fast, too, and I knew I could do all the exercises. When you're as athletic as I am, you're just naturally in pretty good shape. Plus, I work out at home. I'm probably the only girl in Canfield Middle School with her own chin-up bar. (It used to be my dad's, but he never uses it anymore. I use it mostly to keep my arms strong for baseball.)

Maybe Rosie and I couldn't beat the boys in this fitness test, but we were going to give it our best shot.

Eight

Becky and Allie were hogging the porch swing, so Rosie and I sat on the next best place on Becky's porch, the steps. It was too nice a day to spend indoors. I was working on a crossword puzzle, and it felt good to sit there with the breeze blowing through my hair.

"I'm so glad it's the weekend." Rosie sighed. "No more stupid boys, and no more frog cutting."

"Even though I liked being Mark's lab partner—"

"Yeah, I bet you did!" laughed Rosie.

"As I was *saying*," I went on, trying not to smile, "even though it was fun working with Mark, I hated that whole experiment. I hope we never have to dissect anything again."

"I still can't believe Casey captured a live frog and brought it to class," said Allie, laughing.

"If he wasn't such a jerk, I might actually congratulate him."

"Speaking of you-know-who," said Becky, "how are the preparations for his party coming along?"

"Fine," I said. "I called about Melrose Field and they said we could use it next Saturday."

"And we already bought the baseball caps and cards," said Rosie.

I doodled a heart on the back cover of my crossword magazine and filled it in with "J.B. & M.H." It's funny—it wasn't so long ago that I used to write "J.B. & R.C." when I doodled. The R.C. was for Roger Clemens, the great Boston Red Sox pitcher. I'd had a crush on him since my dad took me to my first Red Sox game in fourth grade. But that was ancient history now. Plus, Roger Clemens was a little too old for me.

Rosie leaned over and saw what I had written. "You still have a crush on Mark, even after all this feuding?"

"Yes," I answered shamefacedly. At least Mark hadn't taken part in the feud so far. Maybe he really thought we were gruesome girls, but he hadn't called us names in public yet. I wondered whether he was going to be competing in the fitness test; he had to be, he was a jock. I hoped he wouldn't see me out there, because there's absolutely nothing romantic about the way I look after a workout.

Rosie looked at me with sympathy. "Well, even though he is a beastly boy, he's not as bad as most of them, I guess," she said.

I nodded.

"And you *do* still want him to notice you, right?" asked Rosie.

"Right. But in a good way, not as a dumb girl with braces," I said.

"You mean, you want him to notice how cute you are?" said Rosie.

"Yeah," I admitted. "I'd be glad if I didn't have to worry about blinding him whenever I smiled."

Becky howled with laughter. "Julie, come on!"

"I'm serious, you guys. Have you thought about what it's like to kiss a boy when you wear these things?"

"Julie! Did you kiss someone?" cried Rosie. "You didn't tell me!"

"That's because I didn't," I said. "And I probably never will, at this rate."

"My sister Suzanne says that it's possible for your braces to lock," said Allie suddenly. We all stared at her. "Well, I mean, if both the boy and the girl have braces, that is. You know, they could get hooked together or something while they're kissing."

"That's gross!" exclaimed Becky.

"Allie, have you been asking your older sister kissing questions?" said Rosie. She was giving Allie her special penetrating stare.

"No!" Allie was indignant. "She just told me about it once. She is my sister and we do talk, you know."

"Anyway, it's not true," I added. "Everyone says it is, but it really can't happen. At least not with the kind of braces they have today."

Rosie had begun staring at me in a certain way that I recognized from long experience. She had caught me at something and I knew it. And she knew I knew it. Best friends can be pains sometimes.

"My sister Heather told me about it, too. *Okay*?" I said heatedly. "I wasn't asking her about kissing or anything. She used to have braces and when I got braces I remember she told me about it then. Anyway, the point is I'm never going to kiss anyone, ever. No one is ever going to look at me as girlfriend material because I have these disgusting braces!"

"If it's so important for Mark to notice your looks, why don't you let Rosie give you the makeover she's been bugging you about?" suggested Becky.

"Let her try it," Allie urged me. "You might end up looking like a movie star."

Rosie smiled. "No, I just want to give Julie a . . . well, a more interesting look. So Mark will think, 'Aha! Where has she been all my life?' "

Rosie reads a lot of romance novels, and sometimes she gets a little carried away in real life. Still, it would be great if it worked out like she said. But I wasn't so sure a makeover was a good idea. "I don't know. Won't it just give Casey and the guys one more thing to tease me about? I mean, it's such a girly girl thing to do."

"So what? You're a girl, aren't you? Just because they're being stupid doesn't mean you have to cut off your own nose to spite your face," said Rosie. "Besides, I'm not going to do anything drastic. The effect will be very subtle. No one will even know what's different; they'll just think, 'Gee, Julie looks really good today.' "

I scribbled on the crossword puzzle. "Well, maybe."

"I've got a great idea!" said Becky. "Why don't we do it one day this week, after school? We'll need to get together anyway to go over any last details for the party."

"Yeah, and we can wait and do it after the fitness test, so you guys can concentrate on creaming the boys," said Allie.

I looked at Rosie. "We do have to work out tomorrow and get ready," I said.

"Then it is hereby decided," said Becky in her presidential tone, "that the Party Line meeting is officially switched from tomorrow, Sunday, to the following Thursday—"

"In the interests of beautifying one of its members for said party," Allie continued.

"The treasurer will be responsible for bringing the supplies," said Rosie.

"And we can do it here—in the Oval Attic," declared Becky. "I'll supply the munchies. Secretary, are you writing this down?"

I shook my head. "It is hereby noted that you guys are nuts!" I cried.

Rosie and I spent all of Sunday afternoon practicing for the fitness test. She is a better runner than I am—she runs almost every afternoon before dinner—but I could do a lot more push-ups and chin-ups.

I was exhausted that night, and so I curled up on the daybed, Dizzy on my lap, to read a book on rain forests for a report. My bedroom used to be a storage room. I could share a room with my sisters—they have a huge bedroom, which we shared when we were little—but I like the privacy of my own room. The only thing is, my room is pretty small, and it doesn't have any windows. Rosie painted a poster of a window for me that I have up on one wall. It shows a tree outside, blue sky, and a window sill with a plant on it.

The phone rang, and then I heard my mother say, "Ma! It's so good to hear your voice!"

My grandmother, Goldie, calls us every Sunday night. She used to live in Canfield, but last year she bought a condominium in Florida and moved there. We're pretty close, and I miss her a lot.

After a few minutes my mother yelled up the stairs, "Julie, pick up the phone! It's your grandmother!"

I dumped Dizzy on the floor as I got up. I picked up the extension on the hallway landing and waited until my mother hung up the phone downstairs.

"Hi, Goldie!" I said, settling down on the floor. Dizzy came to find me, and I gently rubbed her back.

"Hello! How's my sweet Julie? Are you engaged yet?"

I laughed. Goldie always teases me about all the boys she thinks are after me. I guess she knows I'm a little boy-crazy. "No, Goldie. But I do like this one guy. His name is Mark. You'd really like him," I said.

"Why?" asked Goldie. "Is he as adorable as you are?"

"He is pretty cute," I said. "And he's so nice, Goldie. He's funny and smart, too."

"But?"

"But what?"

"What's wrong?"

"Well . . . I like Mark, but I'm not sure if he likes me. And I don't know what to do. My friends want to give me this big makeover so he'll notice me, and I'm afraid I'll end up looking like a dork."

Goldie sighed. "Personally, Julie, I think you look terrific just the way you are. You've always been pretty. But you shouldn't be afraid to try something new. Life is full of surprises, you know. Sometimes you just have to take risks."

"What if I look silly?" I asked.

"So? You never looked silly before? But I'm sure you won't. Is this your friend Rosie who wants to give you the makeover?"

"How did you know?" I was really surprised.

"Because, Julie," Goldie said, "I listen to what you tell me. You've told me about Rosie and her makeovers. And remember the last time I visited and you came back from the mall looking like Miss America?"

"You're right. I'll try it." I giggled. "Goldie, I miss you."

"I miss you too, dear. When are you coming to Florida to see me?"

"Soon, I hope. Maybe Rosie and I can come together," I said.

We talked for a while longer, about Goldie's new car and a store she found that has great clothes she wants to buy for me when I go down there. She likes to spoil me, and I don't mind one bit.

Talking to Goldie always gives me such a good feeling. She makes me feel like I really matter to her, and that I can do anything I set my mind to. When I hung up the phone, I was convinced I was going to (a) look beautiful after the make-over, (b) show up the boys in the fitness test, and (c) win Mark Harris's affection.

Grandmothers are great.

Nine

"Come on, Rosie!" I screamed. She was flying down the track in the hundred-yard dash, her wavy black hair streaming straight out behind her. She crossed the finish line way in front of everyone else in her group.

It was Wednesday afternoon, the second and last day of the fitness test. Fortunately, the boys and girls had been separated for most of the events, so we didn't have to deal with a lot of teasing from the boys. But whenever they saw us in the middle of an event, they—Alex, Kip, and Casey, usually—came over and insulted us. We didn't choke, though, not even when I was doing my twentieth chin-up and Casey shouted, "Look at those wimpy arms!" He got in enough trouble from the coach for that, anyway. By then, Rosie and I knew we were going to get our certificates, but we still wanted to show up the boys somehow.

Rosie walked over and joined me in the center of the track. "Nice going," I told her.

She shrugged. "That's an easy race. I can't wait for the mile!"

Leave it to Rosie to prefer four times around the track to one-sixteenth of a lap. I like sports, but running is something I'm just not that good at. If I ever try out for the track and field team in high school, it'll definitely be for the field part. I kind of like the high jump, and I think the javelin would be fun, too.

Different coaches and teachers at Canfield were judging the various events. Rosie and I had the same order of events, but we didn't always compete at the same time because so many kids were involved.

I checked our schedule. "Next is the softball throw," I said.

Rosie groaned. "Well, at least you'll do well in this one," she said.

"I'm not sure I'll be able to beat the guys, though," I said. "They practice a lot more than I do."

"So what?" said Rosie. "Just focus on getting the best girl's toss. It'll still make them mad."

We picked up our sweats and headed over to the football field. On the way, we passed right by the push-up area. Mark was just lowering himself to the ground to start his set. I tugged at the sleeve of Rosie's T-shirt. "Look. Ooh, check out his arms."

Rosie smiled. "They look like ordinary arms to me."

I hit her on the leg. "Well, they're not!" I insisted. "He has nice arm muscles. Look at how skinny Alex's arms are next to his." Then I turned around, casually pretending to scan the track for something, and watched Mark. He must have done at least fifty push-ups, and he didn't even look like he was straining.

"Come on, Julie. We have to hurry," said Rosie. "Put your eyes back in your head."

I giggled. "Sorry."

"Maybe that sight will inspire you to heave the softball all the way to Mars," she teased me.

We reached the football field, where markers were set up in between the yard lines, and checked in with Mr. Griswold, the basketball coach. He told us that we had to throw the ball at least one hundred feet, and we had three tries to do it.

Rosie wanted to go first because she was so nervous. On her first try she got it only to the thirty-yard line. "Come on, Rosie, give it all you've got," I told her. "You can do it."

She picked up another ball, stepped back, and ran up to the starting line. Her throw landed just past the big red marker. The teacher in the

field called out, "One hundred feet, four inches."
She had made it!

"You have one more try if you'd like," said
Coach Griswold.

"No thanks," said Rosie. "I don't think I'll
ever throw anything that far again. Only one
more event left," she said, brushing off her
hands as she walked back to me. "Yeah!"

"Okay, it's your turn," said Coach Griswold,
pointing to me.

I wasn't worried, because throwing baseballs
long distances is something my dad and I practice a lot. You have to be able to throw the ball
far if you're going to play in the outfield. The
only thing is, a softball is bigger and heavier
than a baseball.

I caught the softball Coach Griswold tossed to
me and positioned myself a few feet back from
the starting point. I ran up and just as I was
about to let go of the ball I heard, "Throw it like
a girl!"

The softball dropped out of my hand and went
about ten feet. I turned and saw Casey and his
friends lingering at the twenty-yard line. They
were laughing hysterically.

"Ignore them," said Rosie.

"That won't count as your first try," said
Coach Griswold. "Boys, can we have a little
quiet on the field?"

I was so mad, I wanted to throw the ball at Casey. But I went through the motion again, and hurled the ball as hard as I could. It sailed through the air, and I saw the teacher in the field running backward so she'd be able to see where it landed.

"One hundred forty-seven feet!" she cried out a moment later. "Nice try!"

Coach Griswold noted the distance on my time sheet. "That's better than a lot of the boys have done," he said.

"Really?" I asked.

"Yes," he said.

"That's great, Julie," said Rosie enthusiastically. "Try again."

I didn't throw it any farther on my second or third try. But then, the boys didn't say anything when I tried again, either.

Rosie piled my hair up on top of my head for me and pinned it there so it wasn't hanging down my back. She gave me one of her sweatbands to keep my bangs out of my eyes.

"Thanks," I said.

"Sure," she said. Then she tied her own hair back in a ponytail. In her royal blue T-shirt and white nylon shorts, she looked like a serious runner.

I looked around as I pinned Rosie's number to

the back of her T-shirt. So many people were running in the mile that they had to tell us apart by number. There were some spectators scattered around the bleachers that ran along the long side of the track opposite the starting line. Coach Piper was supervising this event, and people were registering with him.

I saw Mark out of the corner of my eye. He looked great in his black running shorts and black and yellow T-shirt. Rosie pinned on my number, and I began to get really nervous about the race. What if Mark was watching the whole time I was running?

Coach Piper called a group of numbers to the starting line.

"That's us!" said Rosie. When I didn't move, she pulled at my arm. "Don't worry, you look fine," she said.

"Not for long," I added.

"Julie, don't worry so much. You should have more confidence in yourself," said Rosie.

That's easy for you to say, I thought. Rosie was born with confidence. How could I feel good about running a mile with Mark watching me when I wasn't confident that he liked me?

"Okay," the coach called to us, clutching his clipboard. "You're running eight at a time. The track is one-fourth of a mile, so you'll go around four times."

Rosie and I didn't know all the other girls in our heat, but we all smiled at each other. I re-tied my sneakers for what seemed like the hundredth time that afternoon. I looked around the sidelines to see if Mark was still around, but I didn't spot him.

"I'll keep track of your time, so don't think about anything but your running," said Coach Piper. "Now go out there and do your best. On your mark . . . get set . . . go!"

As Rosie and I ran around the long side of the track, I glimpsed some kids in the bleachers. When we circled around and ran past them, I heard Casey shout, "Hey, Rosie! Slow down. You'll never beat the boys anyway!"

Rosie didn't seem to hear him. Nothing can break her concentration when she's running. Still, she might have heard, because she started running even faster.

The third time around the track my hair fell down, but I tried to follow Rosie's example and not let it bother me. I tried to see if Mark was watching, but the one time I did see him, he was talking to Casey.

Rosie crossed the finish line when the rest of us were still on the other side of the track. I had broken away from the other girls, though, so it looked like I was going to get second place in my group. I was glad I hadn't gotten wiped off the track with so many people watching.

When I crossed the finish line, Coach Piper called out, "Nice work, Berger! Seven minutes and eight seconds."

I walked onto the grass and bent over to catch my breath. I was drenched with sweat. Rosie was already standing there with her towel draped around her shoulders. She didn't even look beat.

"How did you do?" I gasped.

"Six minutes and fourteen seconds," she said. "It's not my best, but it's close."

If I hadn't been such a sweaty mess, I would have hugged her. Instead, I jumped in the air for joy. "You're great. Let's go sit down and watch the boys."

Rosie and I pulled on our sweat pants and walked over to the stands. The boys were lining up to run.

Casey and Alex were in the first group, and they came in first and third. Mark ran in the last group; he finished third, but it was a much faster race than the other two because a few ninth graders were competing in that heat.

A few minutes after the last runner came in, Coach Piper shouted, "The results of the mile run will now be announced!"

Rosie and I jumped off the bleachers and walked over to Coach Piper.

"Now, as you know," he began, "anyone who ran a ten-minute mile will qualify for a certificate. That includes almost all of you. In terms of awards . . . Rosie Torres had the best time for a girl, six minutes and fourteen seconds."

I yelled, "All right, Rosie!" and she smiled at me.

"John Ryan had the best time for a boy, with six minutes and eighteen seconds," said Coach Piper, naming one of the boys in Mark's group.

"Rosie, I can't believe it," I said. "You had the fastest time of anyone."

Rosie looked down modestly. "Well, I run every day," she said. "If everyone practiced as much as I do, they could run faster, too."

"I don't care," I said. "I think it's great you came in first. And I don't think just anyone could run faster, either! Even with practice!"

I looked over at Casey. He wasn't smiling.

Rosie and I turned to walk to the locker room. "I can't wait to get out of these smelly clothes," I said.

"Me either," she said. "Race you!"

Then she took off at top speed. I couldn't believe she was running after all we'd done that afternoon. "Wait up!" I yelled, sprinting across the parking lot.

She beat me, as usual. As I opened the door to go inside the school I thought I heard someone call my name.

I turned and squinted at the track. The only person I could see was Mark Harris.

I hesitated for a second. Had he called my name, or was I just delirious? I shrugged and stepped inside the gym.

Ten

We clambered up the stairs to Becky's attic, and Rosie dumped the contents of her canvas bag onto one of the rugs. By the time she'd finished arranging everything, it looked like a mini cosmetic counter. She had everything you could possibly need for a total makeover: eye shadow, blush, mascara, pencils, all sorts of brushes, tiny soft sponges, tissues, special creams, nail polish, fake nails, hairpins, scissors, and barrettes.

"No fake nails!" I said as soon as I saw them.

"Okay, okay," said Rosie. "Take it easy, I'm not going to use all this stuff. I just want to try different things to see what works best on you."

"Is that all your stuff?" asked Allie, goggle-eyed. Allie never wore makeup. Well, hardly ever. Even when she did, it was just a little lip gloss. You could tell she was trying to figure out how anyone could possibly use so many different cosmetics.

"Not all of it," Rosie said, "I borrowed some of it from my mother."

Becky ran up and down the stairs several times while we got ourselves organized. "I made snacks while you guys were running around the track yesterday afternoon," she said.

"But I thought you had to help out at the café," I said.

"I did, but after I cut up all the vegetables for the salad bar, there wasn't anything to do except set the tables, and you know my mom doesn't let me do that!" Becky was notorious for breaking glasses in the restaurant.

"Did you and Mouse have fun yesterday?" Rosie asked Allie. Allie's little brother's real name is Jonathan, but Allie calls him Mouse because the first sound she ever heard him make was a tiny little squeak.

She nodded. "We went to the park. I wish I could have watched you race, though. It sounds like you really surprised the guys."

Rosie laughed. "We did show them a thing or two, I guess," she admitted.

"Her time for the mile was faster than anyone else's. And it was way faster than Casey's!" I said. The official results had been posted outside the gym during lunch.

"I bet he died when he saw that," said Becky.

"It must really bug him. Now he has to admit that girls *can* beat boys sometimes."

"Well, I just hope he's over it by the party on Saturday," said Allie.

"That's only two days away!" I yelped.

"I think we're ready for it," said Becky reassuringly.

"The great news is that Melrose Field has picnic tables and those big stone grills. All we have to bring is the food, cooking utensils, and, of course, the party favors. I don't think there's anything else," said Allie, quickly looking at her checklist. "Nope. We're all set."

"Okay, we've done our Party Line business. Now *our* party can begin." With a flourish, Becky passed around a bowl of nuts mixed with granola, raisins, and chocolate chips.

I grabbed a handful. "So do you think Casey's going to show up at his party?"

"Definitely," said Allie. "He knows better than to throw a party away just to make a point. He's not *that* stupid."

"Yeah, and if all his friends want to go, he won't have a choice," said Becky. "Plus, his mother will make sure he's there."

Rosie was busy setting up her stuff on an old desk. "Becky, do you have a good strong light I can hook up?"

"I'll see." Becky ran downstairs.

"Julie, come sit over here. You know, I should have brought my reflector light," said Rosie, "the one I use for photography."

"Better yet, you should have brought your camera," said Allie. "This is going to be an event to remember." She pulled a cushion up close to watch.

Allie looked so serious, you would have thought there was going to be a test on everything once the makeover was over. Maybe she was thinking of changing her own look and wanted to get an idea of what was possible. Her hair is long and wavy, and she usually wears it clipped back with two barrettes. She's pretty enough not to really need makeup at all. But as Goldie said, everyone should try something new once in a while.

Becky returned with a desk lamp and an extension cord. She plugged in the lamp and tilted it to shine on me. I was sitting on an old piano bench. Then Becky ran downstairs again. When she came back up, she was carrying a pitcher and four glasses.

"I call this creation Perfectly Pretty Punch," she announced.

The rest of us rolled our eyes.

"I named it in honor of your makeover," Becky explained. The punch was red, and it had lemon and orange slices floating in it. "Try it, you'll like it," she laughed. She poured a glass and handed it to Allie.

"Well, here goes nothing." Allie took a sip of the punch. "It's delicious!"

"I'm surprised you didn't call it President's Punch," I said.

Rosie, Allie, and I burst out laughing.

"I don't get it," said Becky.

"Never mind," I said, still grinning at Rosie. We always joke about how much Becky enjoys being president of The Party Line. You know the phrase *born leader*? Well, that's Becky. She'll probably be the mayor of Canfield someday.

"Hand me that Pink Dawn eye shadow, will you, Allie?" asked Rosie. She rubbed a little of it over my eyelids, smoothing it out to the corners. "This makes your eyes look deeper and larger."

"It makes her look like she's been crying," said Allie.

"Thanks a lot," said Rosie, giving Allie an exasperated look. Then she stood back and examined me carefully. "But you're right, Allie, this color might be a mistake. Close your eyes, Julie." She put a cool rose-scented cream on my eyelids and removed the Pink Dawn color with a tissue. "Let's try something gray," she said, "like Dusky Evening." Allie handed her a compact, and Rosie applied it quickly and expertly.

Rosie handed me a mirror. "I look older," I said.

"You're supposed to look older," she said.

"But Rosie, I look like somebody's mother!" I said.

"Hmm, maybe you're right. That color *is* a little dark for you. I'll fix it."

She put another cream on my eyelids. This one smelled sweet, too, but different. I sniffed, trying to figure out what it was.

"This is cucumber cream," Rosie said. "My mom uses it all the time." It felt cool and silky. "How's that?"

"Mmm. I can't decide what's better: the way it smells or the way it feels."

Rosie tried everything on me. After six or seven different eye shadows, four or five shades of eyeliner, brown, black, blue, and violet mascara, and an enormous number of blushers and lipsticks, everyone agreed that my best look was just a tiny bit of pale blue eye shadow to bring out the blue of my eyes and a delicate pink lip gloss.

I had to admit that Rosie had chosen the right colors for me. I still looked like me, only better.

Becky brought up some pastries one of the cooks had given her that afternoon.

"Mmm, this is good," I said, licking the blueberry filling from my lips.

Becky beamed. "They're turnovers. For turning over a new leaf. Get it?"

I laughed. I thought it was pretty funny, even if it was a little corny. Allie just groaned.

"Okay," said Rosie. "Break's over. Now we have to do your hair." She pulled it up to the top of my head and spent about ten minutes arranging it with barrettes and combs. It looked pretty good, but it seemed so complicated.

"Rosie, I don't want to spend this much time on my hair every morning. Can't you think of something easier?"

"Hmm. . . ." Rosie looked at me as though I were a chair she was thinking of reupholstering. Then she unclipped my hair and let it fall to my shoulders again. She pulled it all up to one side of my head and tied it with an elastic band. "What do you think?" she asked. "It's a ponytail, but it's different."

I frowned at my reflection. "I feel lopsided."

Next Rosie tried the same thing, but this time the ponytail came out of the top of my head. It looked cute, but after a minute or two my head began to ache. I could tell Rosie was getting a little frustrated.

"I know what you really need," said Rosie. "A haircut."

"No way," I said, covering my hair with my hands. I'd always had shoulder-length hair, and I liked it that way.

"But short hair is in right now," said Allie.

"Look who's talking!" I cried. "Your hair is longer than mine, and I don't see *you* cutting it."

"Yeah, but I'm not trying to get Mark to like me," Allie calmly replied.

Then Becky started in. "You know, Julie, I think you would look really good with a shorter haircut," she said.

"Read my lips, guys. No haircut."

"Well, okay," said Rosie. "We're not going to force you to do anything you don't want to do. But I think you're making a mistake."

"Really?" I asked.

"Yes." Rosie seemed so sure of herself, and there was no question that she was always right about these things. Besides, I sort of wanted to believe her. "You'll look sensational with short hair. Trust me."

I nodded. Rosie had never given me bad advice before, especially when it came to clothes and fashion. "Maybe you could just trim it a little," I suggested, "so I could get used to the idea."

Rosie smiled. "Sure." She went to get a towel and a glass of water. She draped the towel around my neck, and lined up her scissors, a comb, and the glass of water. I began to get a little nervous. This was beginning to look like a big production.

Rosie combed water through my hair and when it was pretty damp she picked up the scissors. By now I was so jittery I could feel myself shaking.

I heard a tiny *snip* and saw a gigantic bunch of hair fall to the floor. I couldn't believe my eyes. "You're cutting off too much!" I cried.

"Don't worry. I'll be careful," Rosie said.

More hair fell to the floor.

"Julie, don't look so scared. It's turning out great!" said Becky.

I reached up to touch my hair. It didn't even reach my shoulder anymore! "Rosie . . . it's too short."

She stopped and went around to the other side of me. "I just have to even it up," she said. She started cutting on the left side, snipping off a bit here, a bit there. I saw long pieces of my hair fall to the floor. Then Rosie stood in front of me, examining the cut. "Does this look even to you guys?" she asked Becky and Allie.

They stared at me for a minute. "It needs to be shorter on the left side," said Becky.

I jumped up off the piano bench, the towel still around my neck. I shook it, and more hair drifted down. "Where's the mirror?" I demanded. "I want to see it before you cut any more."

Rosie handed me the mirror. Now she was the one who seemed nervous.

When I saw my reflection, I was stunned. I couldn't believe how horrible I looked! "I'm practically bald!" I shrieked. "My hair looks awful! Rosie, you promised me you'd only cut a little! I can't believe how stupid I look!"

My eyes stung and before I could help it, a tear trickled down my cheek. I felt so miserable. How could my best friend do this to me?

Rosie came over and touched my arm, but I shook her off. "Julie, please let me fix it," she said. "One side's longer than the other."

"Just leave me alone! Haven't you ruined things enough?" I said angrily. "I want to go home. Becky, do you have a hat I could borrow?"

One thing about Becky is that she's great in a crisis. She immediately ran downstairs to find something for me to wear. I stood before the mirror with my back to Allie and Rosie. I pulled at my hair, hoping there was some way I could stretch it back to its original length. Maybe I could collect all the hair on the floor and glue it back on. Great. I'd be the only girl in the seventh grade with a wig!

When Becky returned, she had an old sweat-shirt of her brother's. It was a little big, but it had a hood. I wished it were even bigger so I could disappear inside it. I saw the others all whispering worriedly in the corner. Rosie came over and took a deep breath.

"Julie?" she said timidly. She looked like she might start crying, too.

"What?" I snapped.

Rosie blinked, and I saw a tear start moving down her face. "Look, we all feel really bad about this. And . . . we were thinking . . . if you really hate your hair the way it is and you don't trust me to finish it, we'll chip in to take you to a real hair stylist."

"A hair stylist? Do you think anyone will be able to fix this?" I asked.

Rosie nodded, her eyes cast down.

"We can go to that place in the Pine Tree Mall," said Becky. "They're open until seven." It was five o'clock, and the mall was about a twenty-minute walk from Becky's house.

I was still really furious at Rosie, but she looked so unhappy I couldn't bear to make her feel worse. "Okay. Let's go," I said.

Eleven

By the time I left Shear Pleasure, I was ready
to crawl under a rock and hide for the rest of
my life. Dorian, the hair stylist, seemed to know
what she was doing—but what she did was make
my hair even shorter. She even shaved the back
of my neck with an electric razor. Becky thought
I looked like something out of a fashion magazine. I wasn't sure if that was good or bad.

We split up and I hurried home. I was fifteen
minutes late for dinner, and I knew my mom
would be worried about me.

When I opened the front door, she said, "Julie, is that you?"

"Yes, Mom." I walked into the dining room
and Heather started laughing.

"What's so funny?" I asked. I was still mad
about my hair, and my voice came out a lot
sharper than I meant it to.

Heather looked hurt. "I didn't mean anything

by it," she protested. "You just look so cute all wrapped up in that huge sweatshirt."

"Oh," I said, taking my seat. My mother started passing me plates filled with fried chicken, mashed potatoes, carrots, and salad. Everything looked delicious. But I was so upset about my hair and worried about school the next day that I couldn't have eaten if my life depended on it.

"Julie, aren't you at least going to pull back your hood?" asked my father.

I took a deep breath and slipped the hood off my head.

"Wow!" Laurel cried. "That is so cool!" That may sound good, but you have to understand that Laurel also thinks it's cool to shave half your head and dye the rest of your hair blue.

"I like it," said Heather. "It's different."

My mother nodded. "You have such a pretty face—it's nice to be able to see your cheekbones."

I couldn't believe it—they actually liked it! My father even got all sentimental about it. He said, "Well, well. It looks like my little girl has turned into a young lady."

I wondered if anyone who wasn't related to me would like it. Would Mark think I looked even more like a boy now that I had short hair? I could just imagine what Casey was going to say about my hair. I'd never hear the end of it. And we still had that party to give on Saturday.

That night I couldn't fall asleep for the longest time. All the compliments in the world couldn't keep me from dreading school. It was all Rosie's fault! Why had I ever listened to her?

"Julie, won't you even speak to me?" said Rosie the next morning. "It really looks good, you know. You'd get used to it if you'd just give it a chance." She opened her locker, which was only two down from mine, so our elbows were almost touching.

I pulled up the hood of my sweat shirt even more. I could not get used to my new haircut. I never would—not until it grew back to the exact same length it had been before Rosie butchered it. Still, I couldn't bear to make her feel even worse than she did. "It's all right," I mumbled. But I couldn't look at Rosie. I rummaged through my locker for my math book instead.

"See you in the lunchroom?" she said.

"I don't know." I shrugged my shoulders. "Maybe."

"Julie . . ."

"It's not that. I have something I want to do at lunchtime." *I want to make myself invisible,* I added silently.

During lunch period I went back to our homeroom and worked on my reading for social studies. The room was deserted, except for Mr. Reed. He asked me if I was cold and I told him I was, and he left me alone. I had managed to get through most of the morning without any trouble—although Casey had teased me and said I looked like a turtle. I wished I were a turtle. Then I could just hide inside my shell until my hair grew back.

The sixth-period bell rang and I headed for biology class. Kids were swarming through the corridor, and in the jostle to get into the classroom, Casey pushed past me. My hood slipped off!

"I didn't know you were joining the army," Casey said. "Nice crew cut!"

Melinda Wiley gasped when I walked past her desk. She had never seen me with anything but long hair. I just took my seat and stared at the blackboard.

"Psst!" Cindy Sawyer hissed. I turned to my left.

She whispered, "Your hair is—"

I turned back around before I could hear the rest. When Mark walked into the room, I concentrated on organizing my class notes. I couldn't look up and say hello to anyone—not even Rosie, Becky, or Allie.

That class seemed to last forever. I knew everyone was staring at me, and it felt weird not to be kidding around with Rosie. At the bell, Allie handed me a note that read, "We missed you at lunch. Don't worry about anything. You look like a model—beautiful. Meet us after school, okay?" Everyone had signed it.

I nodded, then quickly picked up my books and left the room. Sooner or later I would have to face everybody and listen to all their comments, but not today.

"Hey, Julie!" I heard someone behind me on the stairs yell. I turned around and saw Mark coming toward me. Was he going to make a joke, too?

"You ran off so fast after the race the other day, I didn't get a chance to tell you . . . I mean . . . you were super!" I was so thunderstruck I was rooted to the spot. He took the stairs two at a time and passed me. "By the way, your hair looks great!" he tossed back at me as he disappeared up the stairwell.

I grabbed the railing. Mark Harris liked my haircut!

I ducked into the bathroom on the third floor and stared at myself in the mirror. My face seemed perfectly normal. Sure, my ears showed, but they weren't big. My short hair had a nice shape, and it made my eyes look bigger somehow. When I moved my head, my hair bounced.

There was something about it that was sort of . . . cute. As usual, Rosie had been right.

"Now that your ears show, you need to choose your earrings carefully," said Rosie. She was already back to being my fashion adviser. We were hanging out at her house Friday night, planning my outfit for the party. Mrs. Torres ordered a pizza for the four of us, and we were sorting through Rosie's jewelry box while we waited for it to be delivered. Rosie has more earrings than anyone I know. At last count she had thirty-three pairs.

"I like these," said Allie, holding up a pair of long, dangling ones with small silver hoops and green glass beads. She held them up to her ears. It was funny to see shy Allie with such flamboyant earrings. But then I remembered that Allie's idol, the singer Vermilion, wore long, dangling earrings.

"No, I don't think so," I said. "They're not me."

Becky thought the red-and-white button earrings would look good, but they were too round and solid. They'd look great on Becky, but not on me.

I shook my head. "I think I need something more delicate."

"True." Rosie bit her lip and frowned. She

picked out a pair of small gold leaves—they were real leaves dipped in gold. "Try these," she said. I knew they were her favorite earrings.

"They look so nice," said Becky as I put them on. Allie nodded in agreement.

"They were made for you," said Rosie. She stood back and looked at me, her hands on her hips. "If I give you these to keep, will you forgive me?"

I laughed. "Rosie, of course I forgive you. You're my best friend. And Mark loved the haircut. You don't have to give me your best earrings." I handed them back to her.

She pushed my hand away. "I really want you to have them. To make up for making you feel so awful yesterday. I really didn't mean to cut all your hair off."

"I know that. But why don't you just lend them to me?" I said.

With huge sighs of relief, we hugged each other, and I knew everything was all right again.

"Only twenty-four hours until D-day," Becky reminded us.

"D-day?" repeated Allie.

"Casey's B-day," said Becky, grinning.

"How old is he going to be? Nine?" joked Rosie.

"Who cares about Casey?" I said. "What am I going to wear besides these earrings?"

"I think we should wear our baseball clothes," said Rosie.

"That's a good idea," said Becky. "I'm going to wear my Red Sox T-shirt. It'll match our red caps."

"Do you think I'll look like too much of a tomboy?" I asked.

"This from a girl who wore a ratty old sweatshirt to school yesterday and *still* got a compliment from the boy of her dreams?" said Rosie.

I giggled. "I guess I can't get much worse than that," I said.

"Hey, I don't want to worry you guys," said Allie, "but I just thought of something."

"What?" asked Becky.

"Wait a minute. Where's the list?" I joked. "We need the list!"

"Well, actually, it's something we forgot to put on the list," admitted Allie.

"Not again!" Rosie groaned. "I can't stand working for free, not for Casey Wyatt! No way!"

Allie shook her head. "It's not that. We'll make money from this party. But we forgot to make a backup plan."

"What for?" I said.

Allie stared at me as if I were the dumbest creature on earth. "What if it rains?" she said.

"Oh, no! It can't!" I cried.

"We can't be stuck inside with Casey and his friends. We won't be able to do anything. We won't even be able to make the food the right way," said Becky. She looked desperate.

"I can't believe we forgot this," said Rosie. "I never knew there was so much that went into a party business."

"This is our first outdoor party," I reminded everyone. "It never came up before. But Allie, about that information sheet . . . maybe you should add a space for a rain date or something, just in case."

"I will," said Allie. "But that's not going to help us now." She sounded as glum as I felt. What if we'd done all this work for nothing?

"We could rent baseball videos if it rains," suggested Rosie. "But I can't think of any place big enough for twelve guys and us. I know! Let's check the weather report!" she said.

We all ran into the living room and she turned on the TV. It was just after six o'clock and the news was on.

It seemed like forever before they gave the weather report. The satellite picture showed a big cloud system headed our way, and there were lots of thunderstorms in the Midwest. The cold front wasn't supposed to reach us until

Sunday, but I'd seen enough weather reports to know that the odds were probably fifty-fifty.

Great—one more thing to worry about! I thought to myself.

Rosie sighed as she turned off the TV. "Does anyone know a sun dance?"

Twelve

The first thing I did when I woke up Saturday, even before I opened my eyes, was cross my fingers. When I opened my eyes, light was streaming in my doorway from the window in the hall. So far, so good. Then I got out of bed and went downstairs to check the weather. The sky was a bright, clear blue, and the radio was predicting perfect weather: warm and sunny. Hurray! I rushed back upstairs to take a shower and get ready.

Allie's mom picked me up at about eleven o'clock. She was driving us and all of our stuff over to Melrose Field in her station wagon.

"Julie, I love your haircut!" Mrs. Gray said when I got into the car.

"Thanks," I said. Rosie and I looked at each other and burst out laughing.

Allie turned around and smiled. "Nice weather, don't you think?" she asked me.

"Magnificent," I said. "Boy, are we lucky."

"I was all ready to make up a bunch of rain checks to give the guys when they showed up," said Rosie. "I sketched out a basic design last night after you guys left."

"I'm glad we don't have to use them," said Allie. "It would have been terrible to give Casey a rain check and tell him his birthday had been postponed."

"Why, Allie, I thought you couldn't stand Casey Wyatt," her mother said.

"Yeah, but even obnoxious kids like Casey deserve a fun birthday," said Allie. We all nodded. I love my birthday, and I wouldn't wish that on anybody.

"You're right, Allie," said her mom. "I'm very proud of all of you that you're able to put your feud behind you and behave like real party professionals."

"So what's in all these bags?" I asked Becky. She was sitting in the back, keeping watch over everything so it wouldn't fall over.

"Guess," she said and leaned over, holding one under my nose. The scent of fresh peanuts wafted out. I had a good feeling about this party—finally.

Mrs. Wyatt was already at Melrose Field when we arrived. She was talking to a friend while their children played tag among the trees.

"This is Becky, Rosie, and Allie," I said. "And this is Allie's mom, Mrs. . . uh . . ."

"Jeanne Gray," Mrs. Gray finished. I was kind of relieved, because I wasn't quite sure how to introduce one mother to another.

"I'm pleased to meet all of you," said Mrs. Wyatt, smiling warmly at Allie's mom and then at my friends. "This is my sister, Beth Harris," she said.

Harris? I looked at the woman carefully. She had the same dark brown hair and blue eyes as Mark . . . if she was Mark Harris's mother, then he and Casey were cousins! No wonder they were such good friends.

"Are you by any chance Mark Harris's mother?" I asked. I had to know.

"I sure am," Mrs. Harris replied. "I've heard so much about you girls. I think you're doing a fantastic job."

"Thanks," I said.

"We should probably get to work," said Allie. "It was nice meeting you, Mrs. Wyatt, Mrs. Harris."

The four of us put on our red baseball caps. Becky got the charcoal going in the big stone grill while Allie and Rosie covered two of the picnic tables with tablecloths. I started unloading the supplies. We had two coolers full of canned soda and ice. At least nobody would say there wasn't enough to drink!

The baseball field had been mowed recently, so the diamond was clearly marked. I ran around the bases anyway, to be sure they were clear.

"Way to go, Julie!" called Becky from behind the great puffs of smoke rising from the grill. She had on a long white apron, and she looked like quite the chef. I waved to her.

Rosie and Allie filled little brown paper bags with the peanuts. They set them out on the long table next to boxes of caramel corn.

We were all wearing our Red Sox T-shirts over jeans. With our matching red caps, we looked more like The Party Team than The Party Line.

I was in charge of the game equipment, and I put some gloves and balls over by home plate so the guys could get in some throwing practice before they ate.

"Are you sure you don't need anything else?" Mrs. Gray asked once the car was unloaded.

"Positive. Thanks a lot, Mom."

"Yeah, thanks!" the rest of us chimed in.

"You're welcome," said Mrs. Gray, smiling. "Good luck!"

Cars started driving up about fifteen minutes later. Most of the parents got out, chatted briefly with Mrs. Wyatt, and then left. As each boy arrived, Allie handed him a pack of baseball cards and Rosie added a bag of peanuts. None of them said much—maybe they were a little embarrassed. But I noticed that all of them ripped open their baseball cards and started looking them over, popping peanuts all the while. They were all standing in a group off to one side of the picnic table.

I put on a tape of recent hits. I had mixed in a few baseball-oriented songs, but I didn't want to go overboard. The guys would probably have thought it was queer if I had put on "Take Me Out to the Ball Game," even though I loved hearing it whenever I went to Fenway Park.

Mark arrived with a few younger boys. They each took a bag of peanuts from Allie.

"Thanks," said Mark. "Mmm, these smell good." He waved at Becky. She smiled and waved the barbecue fork.

I knew most of the boys from school, but I didn't recognize the ones with Mark. He led them over to me. "Hi, Julie," he said. "These are my cousins, Jesse and Nick, and this is my brother, Steve." He tugged at the sleeve of the youngest boy, who seemed a bit shy, and pulled him forward.

"Hi," I said. Steve was almost as cute as Mark, but in a little-kid kind of way.

"This is Julie. She's in my class and she's throwing this party," Mark told them. They mumbled hello and then ran off to play. Mark seemed to come from a pretty big family, if you counted cousins.

"Everything looks great," said Mark. "Good idea for a party."

I nodded. "Thanks. It was Becky's idea."

A blue car pulled up at the side of the field and Casey jumped out, followed by his father. Why did he always seem to show up just when Mark and I were starting to talk?

"Hey, guys," said Casey. "How's it going?"

I couldn't believe he didn't make a gruesome girls crack. But I wasn't complaining.

I started fiddling with the cassette player, adjusting the volume. When I turned around, Mark and Casey were over by the baseball stuff.

Casey picked up a ball and glove. He actually looked pretty happy as he walked onto the field. "Come on, guys. Let's go toss a few." The boys pitched to each other for a while, which was great, because it gave us a chance to get going on the rest of the food.

Mr. and Mrs. Wyatt were off on the other side of the field, picnicking with their daughters and Mrs. Harris. I guess they didn't want to spoil Casey's fun.

"The hot dogs are ready!" Becky yelled after

a smoky twenty minutes or so. "Come and get 'em!"

The boys ran in from the field, dropping gloves everywhere. Becky took care of handing out the hot dogs. I showed everyone where the mustard, ketchup, sauerkraut, onions, and relish were. We had two big bowls of Becky's famous Moondance Café macaroni salad. (The Party Line had paid for the ingredients and Becky and Allie had put it all together.)

We also had little bags of potato chips for everyone. I was glad Mrs. Wyatt had warned us that most boys would eat at least two of them. We had a huge supply, but it looked like we'd need it. The boys helped themselves to cold soda.

After everyone else was fed, we grabbed some food for ourselves and sat down for a few minutes.

"It's actually coming off!" said Becky, looking around. The boys were busy wolfing down their lunch, talking and joking among themselves. A few boys were swapping baseball cards while they ate.

"I'm going to get the rest of the equipment for the game," I said. "Can you give me a hand, Rosie?"

Rosie said, "Sure." And then she started clapping!

"Ha, ha," I said.

"Just kidding," said Rosie. "I couldn't resist that."

We went over to the bushes where we had stashed the gear: bats, more gloves, catcher's equipment, and bases, which Allie's brother Mike had provided. I put the catcher's mask on my face to free up my hands and scooped up all I could in my arms. Rosie carried the bats out onto the field.

"Oh no. Girls are *not* playing ball at *my* party!" said Casey. "This is my party, and if I say no girls in the game, I mean it. Get lost."

I dropped the gear and just stared at him through the catcher's mask. I don't know if it was because it was Casey's party or what, but the other boys jumped in and started insulting us, too. The feud was back on, and in full force.

"This isn't a party for girls!" said Elvin.

"Yeah. No women on the field!" shouted Kip.

Becky came running up. She looked so angry, I didn't know what she was going to say.

Allie followed Becky and grabbed her arm. I saw her whisper something.

Becky just turned around and stomped off without saying anything.

"Good comeback!" Casey teased her.

I tried to make peace, for everyone's sake. "Don't get excited," I said. "This game *is* for the boys. I was just getting the equipment out for you. Okay?" I dumped the catcher's mask on top of the other stuff.

At that moment, Mark stood up. "Let's get the game going, Casey."

It looked like disaster had been avoided.

Thirteen

Looks can be deceiving, though.

"Maybe you guys don't mind using girls' stuff, but I do," said Casey, tossing a glove onto the ground.

That did it. I threw my baseball cap down in the dirt. "Casey Wyatt, it just so happens that's my autographed Roger Clemens glove!"

"So what?" said Casey. "You probably don't even know how to use it."

"For your information, I'm a better pitcher than any of you are any day!" I said.

"Oh yeah?" said Casey. "You really think you can beat boys at baseball?"

"Yeah, I do!"

Casey turned to the other boys and laughed. Most of them laughed, too, but a few didn't. Mark was one of the boys who didn't laugh, I noticed.

"Okay," I said. "We challenge you to a game

right now. Let's see, once and for all, if girls aren't just as good as boys."

"All right," said Casey, grinning. "It's your funeral."

Over on the sidelines, Mr. and Mrs. Wyatt were smiling at us. It probably just looked like part of the fun and games to them.

"Are you crazy, Julie?" Rosie whispered. "We can't play them."

"Why not?" I looked at Rosie. She pulled me off to the side, and Allie and Becky joined us.

"Because they'll pulverize us! You're the only one who knows how to play."

"I know we can win, Rosie. You can run, I can pitch, and Becky can hit the ball." I looked at Allie. "And Allie can play right field." Everyone except Allie knows that's where you put your weakest player. She beamed.

"All right," said Becky. "But there are only four of us and there are twelve of them."

"We'll have to get some of the boys to play on our team then," I said. I turned back to the boys. "Casey, can we borrow a few players?"

Casey snorted. "Sure, if you can find anyone who wants to play on a losing team."

"Why don't we pick the names out of a hat?" suggested Allie.

Becky wrote all the boys' names except for Casey's on scraps of paper and tossed them into her baseball cap. Casey was captain of the blue all-boys team, and I was captain of the red coed team.

Becky handed me the cap and I picked the first name. "Alex Wishinsky," I read out loud. Alex groaned and reluctantly left the group of boys to walk over to our side.

"Don't worry, Alex!" shouted Casey. "You won't turn into a girl as long as you don't forget and start playing like one."

Nick Jansen, one of Mark's cousins, and Andy Brodie were picked next. Neither of them looked thrilled. As I reached into the cap for the last name, Mark stepped forward. "I'll be on the red team," he said.

I nearly fell over. "Okay. We each have eight now."

Casey snickered. "Let's play ball!"

"Wait," I said, "we need an umpire, so that it's a fair game."

"I'll ask my dad," Casey said. He ran over to his parents and came back with his father. "Okay?" he said.

"Sure," I said. "Thanks, Mr. Wyatt."

We won the toss, so we were up first. Allie struck out, which didn't surprise anyone, but then Alex struck out and I knew he wasn't trying. I couldn't understand how anyone wouldn't want to play to win.

"Two out!" Casey cried.

Mark was up next, and he connected on the first pitch. With a loud *thwack* the ball went up into the air and landed past second base. Mark made it to first with no problem.

"Okay, Becky, you're up!" I called. Becky had played a lot of softball when she was younger. She could hit with power and she wasn't a bad runner, either.

She swung at the first pitch and hit it right to Jesse Jansen at third base. He caught it easily, and our side was out.

"Sure you don't want to give up now?" taunted Casey.

Kip laughed. "The gruesome girls couldn't even hit the side of a barn if they tried."

"We're just warming up," I told them.

But we didn't do much in the next five innings. Rosie was running her legs off, I was pitching as well as I could, and Becky kept hitting away. The problem was, except for Mark, none of the guys on our team was trying at all. You just can't play with half a team, no matter how good you are. But the other team hadn't scored yet either, so we were still in the running.

In the seventh inning, I had two strikes on Casey and was all set to strike him out when I let a ball get away from me. Casey could tell it was an easy pitch. He took a huge swing and knocked the ball so far over Allie's head that I couldn't even see it.

"Home run!" Kip yelled.

As Casey ran around the bases, he stomped loudly on each one. "I guess it's all over for the girls' team," he said. "Why don't you give up now before it gets any worse?"

"Now, Casey," Mr. Wyatt began. "That's not very nice."

"Sorry, Dad," said Casey. "All right, guys, let's hear it for the blue team!" he cried. A loud cheer went up from the sideline, and I have to admit I was feeling a little demoralized.

Elvin had been on first base when Casey smashed his homer, so two runs scored. I was mad at myself for giving up that home run to Casey, but there wasn't much I could do about it. I just had to focus on the rest of the game.

By the top of the ninth inning I didn't think we had a prayer. My arm was aching up to the shoulder. Mark was up first, and he managed a base hit. Then Becky moved him up to second when she hit a ball to center field that Elvin dropped.

Rosie was up. It was now or never. "Rosie, listen up," I said. "Hit a grounder toward third. You're so fast, you'll make it to first while they're still picking up the ball."

Rosie held the bat firmly in her hands. She ignored Peter's first two pitches. The third pitch was right in the strike zone, and she hit a low grounder right at third base. With a surprised cry, she dropped the bat and ran.

Fred must have been dreaming—or maybe he just never thought Rosie would get a hit. The ball flew right past him. Mark ran to third, Becky advanced to second, and Rosie touched first. Then she kept going!

"Move it, Mark!" Becky yelled.

Mark took off for home plate.

"Where's the ball?" Casey screamed. When Fred finally found the ball, instead of tagging Becky, who was right in front of him, he threw it wildly to home—right over the catcher's head!

Mark, Becky, and Rosie all scored.

"Oh, no!" Casey was holding his head as if he had a headache. "I don't believe this!"

"Yeah!" I cried. We were leading, 3–2.

Allie was jumping up and down. She hugged Becky. "Way to go, Bartlett!"

Rosie and I stared at her. She had never called Becky by her last name before.

"I'm trying to sound like a jock," she said, grinning.

"We're going to beat those stupid boys!" said Rosie.

"What made you run for second?" I asked her.

"You couldn't have known Fred would make *two* errors on that play."

"I couldn't help it!" she said, still panting. "Once I start running, it's hard to stop."

While the rest of our team was up, I wandered over to the bench and found Mark. "Thanks for volunteering to play on our side," I told him.

He smiled. "No problem. Do you think you can hold them off for one more inning?"

I nodded.

"Good. I bet you didn't expect your party to turn into a grudge match, huh?"

"Well . . . actually," I admitted, "I'm not really that surprised."

"Come on, Julie!" cried Rosie. "Time to hit the field!" Both Andy and Nick had struck out, and it was now the bottom of the ninth.

Mark grinned at me as I put my glove back on. "Knock 'em dead, Julie."

I walked to the pitcher's mound in a daze.

Fourteen

I nervously rubbed my arm. If my pitching held up, the game would be over one-two-three. But if I gave them even half a chance, they would wallop the ball. Just knowing that Mark was really on our side gave me confidence, though.

I held the ball the way my dad had taught me, with my index and middle finger across the stitching. Then I planted my feet with my left toe pointing directly at home plate.

Peter Wheeler was up for the blue team. He wasn't much of a hitter, but I wasn't taking any chances. I signaled to Andy, the catcher, that I was sending in a fast ball. I wound up and let it go; it landed smack in Andy's glove. Peter didn't get anywhere near it.

"Striiiike one!" called Mr. Wyatt.

Next I threw a slower pitch, just to confuse Peter. He swung at it and hit a foul ball.

"Strike two!" said Mr. Wyatt.

I tried not to get too excited. "Don't let any-one hit you," I whispered to the ball. Then I threw it as hard as I could.

"Striiiike three!"

Everyone on my team started cheering and whistling, even Alex.

"One down, two to go!" yelled Mark.

Unfortunately, Elvin, who was up after that, tricked all of us with a short bunt. As the ball dribbled toward me I ran forward, but it was too late. The ball reached first base at the same time Elvin did.

"Tie goes to the runner!" Mr. Wyatt ruled.

Fred Lewis, the boy who had made two errors on one play, was the next batter. I threw the ball hard, right in the center of the strike zone. It was so fast it surprised Fred. I threw two more fast ones, and Fred was out.

"All right, Julie!" shouted Becky. "One more!"

I wiped the sweat off my face with my shirt sleeve. I knew who the next person in the bat-ting order was: Casey. Instead of fighting with him again, I pulled myself together and took what my dad calls my battle stance. I looked so hard at home plate it's a wonder it didn't burst into flames. I readjusted my cap and rubbed the ball against the hem of my shirt.

"Nail one to right field!" Kip urged Casey. I

thought of Allie out there trying to catch the ball. I couldn't let Casey hit the ball to her. I couldn't let him hit it, period!

It was easy to send a fast ball past Casey before he knew what had happened. But after that, I didn't have any tricks left. I had a curve ball, but it wasn't dependable. I hadn't used it in a long time. I gripped the ball firmly and threw with all my might.

Casey swung just a millisecond too late.

"Striiiiike two!" Mr. Wyatt called out in a dramatic voice.

Casey turned and looked at his father, who shrugged. "I'm just calling the play," he said.

I took a deep breath. The game could be over with just one more pitch—if it was a perfect one. Casey was staring at the ball in my hand. I was almost afraid to throw it.

Then I wound up and let go.

Casey swung at it, and I heard the crack as the bat hit the ball. My heart sank. Casey threw down the bat and ran for first as the ball arched over the field.

"Alex! Get it!" I hollered.

Alex really tried, but Casey had gotten a good, solid hit. That's the problem with a perfect fast pitch. If the batter's on his toes, he can get a homer off it.

I felt miserable as first Elvin, then Casey were called safe at home.

"We did it!" Casey screamed. "We won!"

I started walking off the field, wishing I could disappear. I didn't dare look at my teammates.

All of a sudden I could feel pounding on my shoulders. It was my teammates thundering around me, cheering and giving me high-fives.

"Nice game, Julie," Alex said shyly. "Any time you want me to be on your team, just ask."

"Ditto," said Nick. He grinned.

"But . . . but we lost," I said.

"Yeah, but you pitched a great game," Mark said.

"It was pretty close, too," Alex said. "We almost made it."

He was right. I looked around me. Everyone seemed like they really meant it, and I knew I had pitched a pretty good game. Too bad it wasn't good enough. I looked over at Casey. His teammates were cheering around him, too. He looked really happy. Well, I told myself, it *was* his birthday.

I knew what I had to do next, but I was dreading it. I started to walk over to shake hands with Casey and congratulate him on a good game. I wanted to prove I could be a good sport. I really meant it, too. He had won fair and square. But I wasn't sure I wanted to hear anything he'd have to say to me.

I had my cap pulled low on my forehead as I trudged toward the winners. All of a sudden I saw a hand stuck out in front of me.

"Good game," I heard Casey Wyatt say. "You guys played great."

Was I dreaming? I flipped my cap up and stuck out my hand. Casey and I shook hands—not for long, but we did shake. "That was some hit," I said. "Two homers in one game is amazing."

"Yeah, thanks," said Casey. Then he shook hands with everyone on my team. "Hey, Rosie," he said, "you should be on the track team next year."

She nodded. "I'm thinking about it."

"Nice hitting," he said to Mark.

"Likewise." Mark smiled. "Happy birthday."

Becky tugged anxiously at my sleeve. "Look," she whispered. "And just when everything was going well, too."

Mrs. Wyatt and Mrs. Harris were making their way toward us, carrying a huge sheet cake with candles. We had purposely left a cake out of the menu because Casey said he didn't like big bakery cakes.

The cake was shaped like a baseball diamond, with little stick player figures on it, bases, and two chocolate bats crossed at home plate. There were thirteen candles on it, and there was a scoreboard made out of licorice strips. It was a really cool cake, and I told myself I'd remember the idea for future parties.

Mrs. Wyatt winked at me. We'd told her why we'd decided against a cake. But I guess she had had more experience than we did with making her kids happy!

She held it in front of Casey, and he smiled. We all started singing "Happy Birthday" at the top of our lungs; I didn't even bother to turn on the tape. Casey blew out the candles on the first try, and we cheered again.

"So how does it feel to be an old man?" Mr. Wyatt teased Casey.

"At least I'm not ancient like you, Dad," said Casey, grinning. His father laughed. I guessed Mr. and Mrs. Wyatt were used to Casey's smart remarks.

Mrs. Wyatt cut the cake and handed it around on the small plates Allie had brought; they featured different major league stars. I looked around and caught Mark looking at me. He gave me the thumbs-up sign. I smiled, and he smiled back.

I looked down at my clothes. I was covered with dirt, and sweat was trickling down my neck. When I took off my cap, I could feel my new hairdo flying every which way. I could almost imagine what Rosie would say about my looks. *She* wouldn't be caught dead looking so messy in front of a guy she liked. She wouldn't even be caught dead looking that way in front of a mirror! I would probably never be as cool and put-together as Rosie, no matter how many makeovers I had. But it didn't bother me.

Mark picked up a piece of cake from the picnic table and walked over to me. "Think you'll be ready to play a rematch next Saturday?" he asked.

"Are you serious?" I laughed.

"Yeah," he said. "Don't you want another chance to win?"

"You bet," I whooped.

"Sure. But be prepared for two out of three if we win the next one. You know how competitive Casey is."

Rosie walked past right at that moment. "Don't tell me we're playing again," she moaned. "I can't take the pressure!"

"Don't worry, Rosie. You'll have a week to practice."

She shook her head. "This is definitely the *weirdest* party we've ever given. Well, see you, guys. I'm going to start packing stuff up." She angled her way through the crowd.

"Want something to drink?" Mark asked me once Rosie was gone.

"Uh, sure," I said. "I guess I better start helping out soon, though."

"You pitched a long game," he said. "You can take three minutes off."

"Okay," I said. We walked over to the cooler and Mark reached in for two root beers. I was so nervous!

We didn't say much while we drank our sodas. Then I said, "Well, I'd better get moving."

"Let me know when Allie's mom gets here," Mark said. "I'll help you load stuff into the car, okay?"

"Thanks!" We smiled at each other, and I walked off with my heart pounding.

Boys can be real pains sometimes, but you know what? Some of them are worth all the trouble.

JULIE'S PARTY TIP
(with a little help from Casey Wyatt's mother)

You don't have to be a jock to give a sports party for boys *or* girls of any age! Just organize a game to take place during the party. Borrow equipment from your family, neighbors, cousins, or school—anywhere you can find it. You don't have to play unless you want to.

But don't forget to keep an eye on the weather, and have another idea in mind, since most parents don't like to have football games in their homes!

Make a birthday cake in the shape of something related to the sport: a football field, a baseball diamond, a tennis court, or a pool, for example. If you don't have specially shaped cake pans, don't worry. You can just cut an ordinary sheet cake into the right shape if you need to. To decorate the top, use chocolate-covered raisins or peanuts for footballs, or licorice sticks for baseball bats. Draw a tennis net with plain white frosting, or color the pool's water blue. It might look funny, but it'll still taste good.

Let your imagination run wild. (But not too wild!)

And don't forget to make tons of food, because athletes eat a *lot*, especially after a game.

Enjoy your party!

Trouble, trouble everywhere . . .
and it's all because of boys

Julie's budding romance with Mark Harris seems doomed. Mark's girl-hating best friend, Casey Wyatt, keeps getting in the way.

Then, in the mix-up of the century, the Party Line gets hired to give a party for Casey Wyatt. And when Casey finds out, it's war!

In a last-ditch attempt to make *something* turn out right, Julie agrees to let Rosie, Becky and Allie give her a daring new look. This means double trouble for the Party Line: Casey hates his party and Julie hates her makeover!

HELP! How will the girls get out of this mess?

Get on

Meet Julie, Rosie, Becky and Allie in this fun-filled series about friendship, growing up, and having a good time!

RL: 4.4

12048

0 71831 00275 4

ISBN 0-425-12048-1

SPLASH™

Rosie's up to something—and she's not telling her friends!

The Party Line!

4

ROSIE'S POPULARITY PLAN

Carrie Austen